YOU GIVE LOVE A BAD NAME

marilyn brant

Twelfth Night
Publishing

(Mirabelle Harbor, Book 3)

DEDICATION & THANKS

For my family, my good friends, and my amazing readers & early reviewers—I adore you all so much!

~*~

Special thanks to Stephanie Littlejohn and Gina Paulus for their wonderful insights on this story before its publication, and to Jennifer Welty for being so kind as to check my French spelling and grammar in advance. I truly appreciated the help! Any mistakes are, of course, my own.

~*~

Finally, my heartfelt gratitude to all of those Eighties-era musicians whose songs still make me smile & dance around the house, even several decades later...

OTHER BOOKS BY MARILYN BRANT

According to Jane

Friday Mornings at Nine

A Summer in Europe

The Sweet Temptations Collection
~On Any Given Sundae
~Double Dipping
~Holiday Man

The Perfect Pair
~Pride, Prejudice and the Perfect Match
~Pride, Prejudice and the Perfect Bet

The Road to You
The Road and Beyond (expanded edition)

All About Us (novella)

The Mirabelle Harbor Series
~Take a Chance on Me
~The One That I Want
~You Give Love a Bad Name
~Stranger on the Shore (coming soon)

Wanderlust in Suburbia and Other Reflections on
Motherhood (nonfiction essays)

NOTE FROM THE AUTHOR

YOU GIVE LOVE A BAD NAME is Book 3 in Marilyn Brant's Mirabelle Harbor series, but this story and all of the contemporary romances in this series can be enjoyed as stand-alone novels.

Also, all of the individual musicians and bands referenced in this novel are real, with the notable exception of Barry Connelly, who is completely fictional, as is his popular love song, "You're the One."

CHAPTER ONE

~*Blake*~

"It's five minutes to the hour at 102.5 LOVE FM," I said into the mic. "But before the clock strikes three and I turn you all over to the capable hands of Amelia Lockett, I've got one more song left to play."

I'd been dreading this. Procrastinating for two hours.

Still, I clicked the song on, and as the opening strains of one of the world's most nauseating tunes hit the airwaves, I said, "This goes out by request to Meggie from Jon—" *Because Jon must be an unimaginative idiot.* "Barry Connelly's classic hit 'You're the One.' Enjoy, young lovers."

I snapped off my microphone, grimaced, and assessed the condition of my booth. My coworker Amelia gave me a saucy smile paired with a mocking thumbs up from outside the booth's window, then she turned back to finish her conversation with Doug, one of our bosses.

As I pulled my keys and my cell phone out of the drawer and set up the automatic playlist that would provide a few minutes of transition time between my time slot and

Amelia's, all I could think was that—across our great northern Illinois listening area—folks were in their homes or driving in their cars or outside enjoying this bright early September day, and they were listening to this crap. Worst of all, it was my fault.

Barry Connelly's lyrics couldn't have been stupider. And I was actively contributing to the dumbing down of American society just by agreeing to play his songs. Who could possible *like* this sentimental shit?

"My love...you are like starlight in a moonless sky," Barry crooned.

"Your arms...wrap around me and the moments just fly.
Your eyes...pierce into my soul and leave me undone.
And your lips...ooooh, baby, ooooh, baby, you're the one."

Kill. Me. Now.

The chorus was so sappy I needed a freaking shower to wash off the stickiness.

Finally, after about four years worth of "ooooh, babys," it came to a merciful end.

I clicked my mic back on, summoned every ounce of sincerity I could muster, and said, "That's some...um, inspired songwriting, eh?" I'd been doing my best to keep the sarcasm out of my voice, but Doug must have heard it anyway because he shot me a warning look through the glass. I faked at grin at him and added, "Blake Michaelsen signing off for this afternoon. Have a wonderful Labor Day and remember, with 102.5, we've got 'Nothing but love, 24/7,' so stay tuned for more romantic hits."

I switched on the transition playlist, slammed down my headset, and snatched my keys and my phone.

"All yours, chickie," I said to Amelia, who slugged my chest as we traded places.

"Don't call me that, you douchebag," she said, and then affectionately flipped me off.

I made a reciprocal rude gesture, just to make her laugh,

and then blew her a kiss. "Hey, have a good afternoon."

"You, too, Blake." She waved. "'Til tomorrow."

Yeah.

There were no holidays in broadcasting.

Labor Day. My birthday. An unremarkable Monday. You name it, we worked it.

The radio station, however, was not the worst that was in store for me today. My sister Sharlene and my sister-in-law Olivia had colluded in their Machiavellian way to fill up every possible open afternoon with a family gathering of some sort, whether it was Labor Day, my birthday, or an unremarkable Monday.

Turned out, today was all three.

Doug tossed me the keys to the white van as I exited the booth, along with a wary glance, like I might just be dangerous if confronted. He wasn't half wrong.

"The equipment is already packed in there, and the GPS is set. You just need to drop the stuff off for J.J. before four."

"Not a problem," I assured my boss. "But I have to go straight to a family event right after that, so is it okay if I return the van this evening?"

"As long as you don't crash it," Doug said with a laugh, although I could tell he wasn't entirely joking. He'd probably read that I'd had a few fender benders in the past couple of years. They put everything in that damn *Mirabelle Harbor Gazette*.

"I'll bring it back undented and in one piece," I promised. But I had to admit, once I was in the driver's seat and had the ignition on, the rev of the engine made me want to floor it. How fast would this white whale go on the open road?

I swung by my apartment, just a block away from the station, to pick up Winston. I'd gotten him from the shelter only about two weeks ago—a one-year-old Havanese/Cocker Spaniel/Poodle/who-knows-what-else mix with insecurity issues. But we understood each other, and he already felt like the best roommate I'd ever had.

I scooped him up and took him to the van. Immediately he started sniffing the portable speakers in the back. He raised one stubby caramel-colored leg to mark his territory.

"Dude, they're Bose speakers. Don't pee on them." I laughed and he paddled toward me.

Hyper ball of fur, but funny as hell.

"J.J. would be ticked if he couldn't use them tonight," I informed my dog. "Not to mention the rest of the sound system for his gig." I pointed at the boxy equipment that we sent out for on-location events, like the private retirement party J.J. Jones was hosting for his neighbor this evening.

Winston cocked his head to one side, looking back longingly at the speakers. He barked.

"Tempting, I know, but why don't you join me up here instead?" I patted the passenger's seat and he jumped up on it. Got comfortable. Winston liked going for drives. It relaxed or soothed him or something.

And what could I say? I liked having him with me for the same reason.

On the round trip up to the suburb of Libertyville and back, I told him about my day. It didn't feel like I was talking to myself when Winston listened so attentively and barked at reasonable intervals in response.

"Can you believe that jackass?" I asked him as I gave the idiot in the blood-red Camaro the finger. "You saw him cut me off, right?"

Winston barked.

"I thought so," I said, once again tempted to floor the gas pedal and see how fast I could get this tank moving on Route 45 South. But the jackass sped through a very yellow light, and I wasn't dumb enough to follow him. At least not this time.

Instead, I just pounded on the steering wheel and glared hard at the Camaro's tires, willing them to run over a random nail. Would serve the bastard right.

Winston hopped off the passenger's seat while we were stopped and put his head into my lap, expecting to have his ears rubbed. And the second I touched his curly fur, I felt a little better. I didn't even order him to return to his seat when the light turned green again and we approached the Mirabelle Harbor city limits.

"So, what d'ya think, little guy? Should we drive around a while more, kill another half hour, or head directly to the party?"

Winston glanced up at me with huge brown eyes and made this plaintive, throaty sound—part growl, part moan. He wanted to stay right where we were and continue to get petted.

"I know exactly what you mean," I assured him, "but we both know there's no way my sister will let me get out of this. The good news is that you'll have a big yard to run around in for a few hours. And there will be squirrels."

Winston's ears perked up. Pretty sure he recognized that word.

This latest Michaelsen family gathering was being held at my elder brother Derek's place, which he shared with his wife Olivia and my three young nephews. It also happened to be the house where my siblings and I all grew up. A beautiful brick home on Lake Michigan, originally built by my grandparents in the late 1930s. It had been in our family for three generations now. When our parents died a few years back, Sharlene, Chance, Chandler, and I were in unanimous agreement that the house needed to stay in the family, so we made it easy for Derek and Olivia to buy us out. Hopefully one of their sons—James, Riley, or Peter— would be the next owner.

As we pulled into the long driveway, I saw that my youngest brother's Jeep was already there. No doubt Chance's girlfriend Nia was with him. The two of them were joined at the hip these days.

His twin, Chandler, had been roaming around the country since Mom died and was currently in Georgia (or so I was told). He wouldn't be here.

And I didn't see Shar's car, which, since my sister was unerringly punctual, meant she probably walked over from her friend Julia Crane's place. My sister was house-sitting this weekend while Julia and her daughter were out of town, and their home was only a few blocks away.

In other words, Winston and I were the last to arrive. As usual.

I walked—and Winston trotted—around to the backyard. Most of our picnics were held on the back patio, unless the weather turned sour.

Shar saw me first. "Surprise," she said dryly, and pointed to a large chocolate birthday cake on the outside table.

I rolled my eyes at her.

"We know you hate surprises," my sister retorted, "so we just made you a cake, which I'm sure you expected. So, it's not really a surprise."

"Thanks," I said. I did expect a cake and was grateful there seemed to be nothing else out of the ordinary. One year, Chandler thought it would be a good idea to hire a private exotic dancer as my birthday present. That *was* a surprise. While I found the whole thing kind of hilarious, actually (especially Shar and Olivia's shock when the dancer started twirling around the living room in little more than a few sheer veils), my girlfriend at the time was less than amused. We broke up two days later.

"Happy Birthday, man!" Derek said, walking over to greet me and shaking my hand. "Thirty-five. You're getting old."

"Fuck you," I said cheerfully. "And it's not for another hour and fifty-three minutes." Not that I was counting or anything.

He laughed. "Close enough."

Derek was three years older than me and getting dangerously close to forty. But then, considering he had a wife of almost twelve years and three children, he had a lot to show for it.

"Can I get you a beer?" my big brother asked.

"I might have to hurt you if you don't."

He laughed again and reached down and ruffled the fur on Winston's head. "I've got some tasty scraps for you, boy."

Winston wagged his tail and set off on a beeline for the nephews, who were playing some kind of Frisbee-tag game with Chance and Nia in the middle of the yard. My kid brother and his girlfriend waved at me, but they were preoccupied with the little rugrats. Chance, who was twenty-eight and a professional personal trainer, had made it his mission to make sure James, Riley, and Peter got their daily recommended level of physical fitness minutes. He was kinda fanatical about it.

My sister-in-law ushered me over. "Have some chips and salsa while Derek finishes the grilling," Olivia said. "And fill us in on what's been going on."

Derek handed me a cold bottle of beer, which tasted like heaven after the stress of the workday, and Olivia and Shar settled back in their lawn chairs and waited for me to entertain them.

I launched into a few stories about my coworkers at the radio station—Olivia always loved that—and then added a few Winston tales, which made Shar smile. By the time my birthday burgers were ready, I'd had another couple of beers and was feeling almost relaxed. I always thought it fitting that I'd been born in the middle of Happy Hour.

"Come here, boy," Derek called to my dog, waving some ground beef and a strip of bacon at him. He bounded toward us like a shot.

As Winston gobbled up the meat treats, my brother laughed. "Different breed I know, but this little guy's eagerness reminds me of Zeus. Remember how much he loved his food?"

Yeah, I remembered.

I nodded.

Derek chuckled. "You ever think about him? Looking back, I wouldn't be surprised if you were his favorite."

I didn't begrudge my brother for living in our family home, gorgeous and spacious as it was. For me, it would have been torture. The place was a minefield of memories, many of them happy, but a hell of a lot that were heartbreaking, too.

"I still think about Zeus. Still miss him," I admitted, although I didn't confirm that I was our golden retriever's favorite, even though I knew I was.

Since grade school, I'd cried exactly three times. At the funerals of each of my parents and when we had to put Zeus to sleep. I'd just turned fourteen when it happened, and it felt like I'd lost a sibling that day.

My brother called over Chance, Nia, and the boys. "Time to eat, everyone!"

The crew rushed to the patio, and I got several more birthday wishes, hugs, and back slaps.

Little Peter, who was five and had just started kindergarten, wrapped his wiry arms around me and squeezed. "Happy Burffhday, Uncle Blake."

"Thanks," I said. The kid had a little trouble with his "th"s, but he was so damned cute. Not that I wanted to be a parent or anything. I shuddered just thinking of the responsibility.

As we fixed our burgers and dug into the potato salad, fruit, corn on the cob, and a bunch of savory Greek pastries that Nia had brought in (her family owned the Greek restaurant and bakery in town), the Michaelsen women regaled us with the latest Mirabelle Harbor gossip.

"Marianna Gregory is *still* in Sarasota!" Olivia began.

"What?" Shar said. "But I thought she was only

planning on staying until—"

"She *was*," Olivia interrupted. "But then I got this phone call from her and, oh, my goodness. I have to show you some of the pictures she sent. She emailed a bunch of them to me last week and—"

"Another beer, Blake?" my brother Chance asked. The guy was such a health nut that he didn't drink much, but he looked even less riveted by the Floridian adventures of our sister-in-law's good friend than I was. And that was saying something.

"God, yes," I told him.

Undaunted, Olivia kept yammering about what Marianna had been doing in Sarasota this summer. Not to be outdone, Shar then launched into this seemingly endless tale about what *her* BFF was doing out in California this weekend. I knew Julia Crane slightly better than I knew Marianna Gregory, and I also knew about the tragic death of Julia's husband last year, so it wasn't that I felt unsympathetic. It was just that I had a hard time following all of the details and the sheer number of people involved in these meandering stories. But, hey, if Julia and Marianna were happy, I was happy for them.

Thankfully, Nia didn't have any gossip to contribute to the discussion—then again, she wasn't a Michaelsen woman. Yet. That was only a technicality, though. A matter of time.

I looked over at Chance, who couldn't seem to take his eyes off of her. Man, he was so whipped. I cringed, but I knew it was what he'd wanted. Still, the guy wouldn't make plans for *anything* anymore without checking with Nia first.

Fortunately, the force of their attraction seemed mutual, which was a good thing. I would have been royally pissed if she'd been out to break his heart. He was just so smitten. I'd never seen Chance like that.

It made me feel all the more like a loser, though. An

aging one at that.

My little brother got up to throw out his paper plate and kissed his girlfriend en route.

"You know I've got the big 102.5 van in the driveway if you two need some, uh, privacy," I said.

Nia blushed, and Chance looked around only long enough to make sure the kids were out of earshot before he said something uncharacteristically impolite to me.

I held up my hand in a show of surrender. "Hey, just offering," I said. "I know how young love can be." And everyone laughed. But it only reinforced what I fraud I was. Talking about love like I knew what I was saying. Playing love songs every damn day and never believing a word of them. Other people could meet and fall in love. Not me.

Shar caught me contemplating this and murmured, "Be kind to them. It's true love."

"Did I look like I was gonna say anything else?" I retorted.

She shook her head. "That's what worries me about you today. You've made a few wisecracks, but you've been unusually quiet for you. Almost somber."

"I'm not somber. You always exaggerate."

"I *always* exaggerate?" she mocked. "Yeah. Are you being purposely ironic or just accidentally thickheaded?"

I sighed. "It's my fucking birthday. You're supposed to be nice to me today."

"I *am* being nice to you. Tough love, Bro." She poked me in the side of my neck with her index finger.

She'd done stuff like that for as long as I could remember. We were toddlers together. I was just a couple of years older than her, and she was forever jabbing at me. It didn't hurt, but it pissed me off. Enough so that I got up and stalked off to a distant corner of the yard. She followed me.

"What's on your mind, Blake? I know something's bothering you."

Fine. If she was going to pester, I'd let her have it.

"Look, I'm in a bad mood and tired of people telling me how I should act and which words I should say and what I should believe. I'm glad Chance and Nia are happy, and I think it's great that Derek and Olivia have stayed together all these years. But they're the exceptions not the rule. I think love is an unrealistic aspiration for most of us." I shot her a significant look and she flinched as if I'd slapped her. Her ex-husband Stephen was a cheating scumbag. She knew it. I knew it. And the entire family knew it. "Sorry to bring up a painful subject, Shar, but you know as well as I do that not everyone gets a happily ever after ending."

She bit her lip and her eyes got a little watery. I felt like a tool for upsetting her, but I had to make my point clear. "For me, true love is a myth. I'll be the first to admit it if I ever change my mind, but that's not likely."

"Maybe we've just been unlucky," my sister whispered. She stared longingly at our two brothers across the lawn and the ladies in their lives. "Maybe everyone has the *potential* to fall in love, but they just have to find the right person. Find their exception to the rule. Maybe our perfect match isn't who we think it should be."

I shook my head and half smiled. "I love you, Sis. I really do. But I think you're full of romantic bullshit. Like all of those people who listen to that dopey Barry Connelly."

"I like Barry Connelly's songs," Shar said.

"Of course you do."

She swiped at her eyes and gave me an evil little-sister glare that was, actually, kind of endearing. "You're a real dickhead, Blake. Which I say lovingly."

I snickered.

Then she speared me with her index finger again, this time on my shoulder, just as Winston came flying over to us.

"What? Did the squirrels not want to play?" I asked my

dog.

Winston just rolled on the grass in front of me, waiting for one of us to rub his belly. I bent down and did the honors.

Shar, who looked as though she were about to say something else, gave me a funny glance and, instead, just crossed her arms.

"Now what?" I asked. "Have you figured out something else that's wrong with me?"

She nodded. "You're such a liar. Winston is proof that you have a heart after all. Deep down. Just look at the two of you. He's good for you, as dumpy and skittish as he may be—"

"Don't insult my dog."

She raised a knowing eyebrow. "He takes you out of your cynical bachelor head for at least a few minutes every day. It's not long enough, but it's a start."

"Oh, stop acting all superior, like you know me better than I know myself." Argh. *Sisters*.

"I've known you for almost all of your thirty-five years. I'd say I have a greater insight than most." Shar drew herself up to her full height, which was a good six inches shorter than me. However, though she seemed small, I knew she was mighty. She added, "Now come over to the picnic table and eat a piece of your damn birthday cake or you'll be wearing it home."

I grinned. She wasn't kidding. I knew from the teasing expression on her face that she, too, remembered the time in grade school when she'd made me pudding. She felt I "needed" it. I'd been in bed sick and told her I didn't want it. The minute my fever was officially gone, she gave me another chance to do what was good for me. When I still didn't eat it, she dumped a bowl of it on my head. To this day I couldn't look at butterscotch pudding without thinking about her.

"Just watch yourself, Shar. Not everyone will put up

with your temper, your lectures, and your stubborness like I do."

"Don't I know it," she said, unable to disguise the hint of sadness in her voice. Then she snapped her fingers at Winston. "You come, too, you big cutie. I've got a dessert for you, as well."

And my traitorous little dog jumped up and away from me and followed my sister without question.

I dropped the van off at the radio station first and then an exhausted Winston at my apartment. Between my nephews and a yard full of squirrels, he'd run himself ragged. I watched him drag his furry body over to his water bowl, slurp up a few sips, and then collapse into a heap on the cool kitchen floor.

Much as I wished I could do the same, my mind just wouldn't shut down. It kept racing from one thought to the next, but most of the thoughts were variants on the same theme: I was now officially thirty-five years old, and what did I have to show for it?

I was single and the definition of the kind of guy who was a drunk girl's one-night stand.

I lived in a small apartment with a scruffy dog I'd picked up on a whim.

I dressed like an overgrown college kid all the time in jeans and t-shirts because I knew no one on the air could see me.

Even though I had degrees in two different fields—communications and marketing—I'd quit a bunch of jobs because they were boring, and I wasn't exactly advancing in my new radio career because love songs annoyed the shit out of me. (Try to explain *that* on a resume.)

When had I gotten so stuck in this rut?

When did I become a boring, thirty-something fool whose only Rx was the typical slacker combo of bar babes, alcohol, and mind-numbing TV?

Seriously. It was depressing as hell.

Also, these habits were hard to break.

I left my apartment and my dog and found myself heading toward the nearest bar in Harbor Square, like a magnet drawn to its mate.

There were two main drinking establishments downtown, not more than two blocks from my apartment complex, and they were next to each other: A newish wine bar for hipster types called The Lounge (Shar and her friends liked it), and a *real* bar that had been in the square for years—Max's Pub, a sports bar where everyone knew my name.

I meandered inside Max's and squeezed into a space at the bar counter. Football was on. The Chargers versus the Broncos. Couldn't say I cared about the game. It was the Bears or nothing for me. But I had my attention split between Gina, the smokin' hot bartender who was wise enough not to let me pick her up (I'd tried a dozen times), and the top shelf vodka I liked to drink straight on nights when I was feeling especially sorry for myself.

"How are you doing, Blake?" Gina asked, all smiles. As it got later, the guys in the room got drunker and they tipped more freely.

"I'd be better if you came home with me," I said. "When's your shift end?"

She laughed. "Too late for you. You'll be wasted in an hour."

I checked my watch and shrugged. "Ah, you're probably right."

"I know I am."

"Is that why you never let me pick you up? I mean, I could stay mostly sober tonight if you wanted me to wait for—"

"Blake," she cut me off, "You know I think you're a sweetheart...usually, but I'm not looking for a fling." She patted my head like a Sunday school teacher might. "But don't you worry. I know you'll find plenty of women who are looking for just that. I've seen you go home with enough of them."

"Ow. That sounds an awful lot like an accusation."

"Well, I'm not your sister. I don't have to be nice to you."

"Have you ever *talked* to my sister? 'Cuz then you'd know she isn't all that nice to me."

Gina laughed. "Careful. This is a small town. That might get back to Sharlene."

I grinned at her. "I can only hope."

But despite my attempts to flirt with the bartender, she had other customers to attend to, and I was left with my vodka and my loneliness.

I glanced out the window and saw a bunch of local teachers approaching the front entrance to The Lounge. I recognized a few of the women from around town. Since Shar was an English teacher at the junior high, she'd introduced me to a number of fellow educators over the years. Teachers were generally too straight-laced to be my type, though, so I never paid much attention. The only one in the crowd tonight whose name I even remembered was the French teacher, and she taught at the high school.

Vicky.

I'd seen her at the radio station when I was doing a big interview with actor Dane Tyler this summer. I distinctly remember Shar saying that Vicky was single.

"Need another?" Gina asked me.

"Maybe just one or two more." My head was finally starting to catch a decent buzz, so I should have been feeling a lot better, especially after Gina gave me a freebie drink in honor of my birthday. But I was still irritated. Thinking about the radio station made me think about those sappy love songs. Whether the musician was pouring his heart out about "love gone wrong" or the joy of "the first time," it didn't matter. I couldn't stand either extreme.

Those songs were the worst kind of subversive lie out there. And people just accepted whatever the singer sang as truth because it was delivered in harmony and with lyrics that rhymed. Idiots.

But I knew the real truth. Love wasn't a panacea for all of life's ills.

No.

Love made everything worse, at least for most people. Love made everyone it touched vulnerable. I'd witnessed it firsthand, time and time again. I'd seen that vulnerability nearly level my strong, smart sister when her ex cheated on her. I'd watched two out of my three brothers wrestle with their sense of self worth when trying to win the women in their lives. And I'd had a front-row seat as my mother suffered through the early death of my father from stomach cancer, and she never really recovered. Her stroke a couple of years later was a shock to most of my siblings, but not to me. Her weakness in the face of love had incapacitated her. Made her feeble. She didn't have the will to keep fighting anymore.

I had no intention of putting myself in a position like that. Not ever.

I raised my glass to take a big gulp of my third (or, maybe, fourth?) vodka when a human brick wall slammed into me.

"What the fuck?" I yelled as alcohol dripped down my face and splashed into my eyes. Damn that stung. "Watch where you're going, asshole."

"Who are you calling an asshole, you asshole?" the brick wall yelled back. Not too witty, this one, but there was a feral look in his eyes.

And even through my vodka haze, I recognized four definitive things about the other guy:

1. He was at least as wasted as I was.

2. He was at least twice my size—which was impressive because I wasn't a little man—but this dude was wide and thick-necked, like a linebacker.

3. He was at least a decade younger than I was. A college football player, maybe?

4. And he was at least as argumentative as I was, which let me know that we both wanted the same thing. Had a similar need. The taste for real blood...our own. Something to distract us from the internal pain by replacing it with a physical one.

I shoved him back. "I'm calling *you* an asshole. Get outta my face."

"No, you fuckin' prick."

I met his gaze and he was laughing at me. His bloodshot eyes pleading with me to land the first punch so he could batter his knuckles against my jaw.

I threw down my glass, shattering it, and pushed my way to standing. Gina yelled, "Take it outside, guys! Right now, or you'll be tossed out!" A pair of bouncers appeared out of nowhere.

The brick wall pointed to the door.

I pointed, too. "After you, dickhead."

He lifted me up by the nape of my t-shirt and half-shoved, half-hauled me out of the sports bar. A group of guys, probably his friends, followed us out. They were shouting a bunch of shit that I couldn't focus on. The dude was bigger and he was stronger, but I was faster, and I managed to land a couple of blows before his first slammed into my stomach, stole my breath, and literally brought me to my knees.

With me so low the ground, I could grab at his legs to try to slow him down, but it was just a delay game, and we both knew it. He rained punches down on my head like a hailstorm. But through the pain, I was calm. All I had to think about was survival, not living. And for the few moments the fight lasted, it was a relief.

But then someone pulled him off me and dragged him away. I caught sight of a police officer's uniform, some yelling, and a quickly dispersing crowd, including those teachers who were at the wine bar next door. Vicky, that babe of a French teacher, was one of them. As I spit out a mouthful of blood, I caught her staring at me. It was a look of pure disgust.

Well, screw her.

The cop approached me, but I didn't look at him. It wasn't until he said, "What are you doing, Blake?" that I recognized the voice.

I'd known Terrance Ryland since second grade. He was black, well built, and bullshit free. I winced, more from embarrassment now than bruises.

"Hey, T," I mumbled.

"Officer T to you," he said with a hint of a laugh. "You need to go home. Now."

"I know. I'm going."

"Do you need help getting there?" he asked me.

I shook my head, and the world spun in a wild arc. "I live nearby."

"Well, go right home then, Blake. I can't have you out here disturbing the peace. I don't want to have to bring you in, but I will."

There was no mistaking the seriousness in his voice. A genuine warning.

"I hear ya." I forced myself to sober up enough to stand up straight and take a stride or two away from him.

"Are you sure you're okay?" Terrance asked, softer this time.

"I will be. I just need some sleep. And, maybe, a few bandages."

He chuckled. "You haven't changed one bit since elementary school. Always at the center of a brawl. Take care of yourself, okay? And, please, stay out of trouble."

"I'll try," I said. But I was lying.

I walked away from Harbor Square until I was out of the cop's view, then I hugged the wall in the alley between the art gallery and the liquor store, needing it to hold me up. I paused to puke into the gutter.

"Pathetic," I heard someone muttering as they walked by. Or maybe it was just the voice in my head, commenting on my personal state of being.

Somehow I managed to stumble the final block home, and Winston greeted me at my apartment door, tail wagging.

His joy in seeing me filled my heart with a gratitude I knew I didn't deserve to feel. As I let him out for his last doggy break of the night, I almost broke down right there in the doorway. Here was a creature who loved me without conditions, even in the shitty, drunken, beat-up state I was in. No woman would ever have half of the love and respect for me that this little mutt did. I knew that for sure.

But after we returned to the apartment, that was the last coherent thought I had before I patted Winston's soft head one more time, collapsed onto my sofa, and blacked out until morning.

CHAPTER TWO

~*Vicky*~

"I'd been out with my teaching friends from the foreign language department, drinking wine at The Lounge on Monday night, when I caught sight of my Dream Man.

"Oh, just look at him," Lisa, our resident high-school German teacher, said in that swoony voice she usually reserved for pictures of hot firemen on Facebook. "I just want to run my fingers through his dark wavy hair and unfasten that cravat." She paused to tilt her phone and zoom in on the image. "And touch his legs. In those tight breeches—"

Marcie, who taught French with me, snatched the phone from her. "Let me see that." She silently analyzed the photo then nodded. "Yeah. *Il est parfait.* He's perfect. His hair. His figure. And he can pull off the period costume without looking like a total dork."

Janet, who was in her tenth year of teaching upper-level Spanish, wrestled the phone away from her and held it so that Christine, also in the Spanish department, and I could finally see the picture. The three of us leaned in to study the

Entertainment Monthly website and read the article below the photo, which featured an "intimate first look" at the actor cast to play Mr. Darcy in the latest British film adaptation of *Pride and Prejudice*.

"Professionally trained at the Royal Shakespeare Theatre," Janet read. "Studied dance, art, poetry, fencing, and voice."

"A longtime Londoner and a vegan," Christine added, sounding impressed. "He got his start on the stage, had a walk-on role in the BBC drama *Poldark*, has been on *Masterpiece* a number of times, and starred in a touring musical production of *The Scarlet Pimpernel*." She read further. "And—whoa, he's even made a guest appearance on *Downton Abbey*."

Everyone at our table squealed.

"How did I miss that episode?" Lisa asked.

I finally got a closer look at the picture. Gareth Wellington was gorgeous, well read, and clearly talented. Too bad he wasn't *actually* Mr. Darcy. Or a man who lived within a reasonable driving distance of Chicago. Or even single.

"He has a husband," Janet said with a disappointed sigh. "From Stratford-upon-Avon."

Of course he did.

All the good men in the world were either gay, taken, or fictional.

We talked for a little while longer about English, Scottish, Irish, and Aussie actors and the hotness of their accents before we moved on to the classical concert series that had just ended at the Parkside Pavilion, an orchestra hall nearby. Then Janet mentioned something about an upcoming tapas tasting at the Flamenco Grill and our discussion turned toward Spanish appetizers.

I found myself laughing louder than usual, although I'd always enjoyed my visits to the wine bar. Even the times I'd been here with the Quest group, a local singles' club I'd gotten roped into joining, had been fun.

But it was better getting to go out with my teaching friends.

They were all into cultural things, too—from imported cheeses to foreign-language films and international music, from exotic cuisine ideas to world literature and European travel—so I didn't have to explain myself to them. They loved watching *Masterpiece Theater* and reading classic novels (in more than one language, even). But, mostly, it was just such a relief to be able to relax when I was with them and not worry about dating. Not have to try to sell my romantic and girly self to some guy who'd just grunt and find my infatuation with flower gardens, French pastries, and Regency-era clothing laughable.

I knew I was well on my way to becoming one of those spinster types who read the English author alphabet (Austen, Brontë, Chaucer, Dickens...), drank tea, and talked mostly to my cat. But what could I do? It was what I liked.

And it wasn't really as lonely as it seemed. Anything was better than the alternative—being in a relationship with a man who didn't *get* me. My friend Sharlene and I had talked about that after the last Quest outing. She'd been married and divorced already, which made her all the more cautious, but after my series of harsh breakups, I'd take a fictional BBC hero over a flesh-and-blood American male any day.

"Hey, I should be leaving soon," Christine said. "It's going to be a long day tomorrow."

I nodded and started collecting my things. Since she was driving me back to my apartment, that meant goodnight for me, too.

"The students are always so hard to manage after a three-day weekend," Marcie said, frowning as she checked her watch.

"Yeah, we should all go home and get some sleep," Lisa agreed.

So we settled our bill and stepped outside of The Lounge just as a ruckus was getting started next door at Max's.

"You asshole!" this dopey, burly, drunk guy screamed, ineffectively swinging at another drunk guy.

"You witless dickhead!" slurred the second guy. But that didn't mask his identity. As soon as he spoke, I knew who it was. Everyone did.

"Isn't that Blake Michaelsen?" Janet whispered.

"Yep," I whispered back. I'd only seen him in person once before—at a big event at the radio station this summer—and it was, literally, across a crowded room. But Blake's voice on 102.5 LOVE FM was one of the sexiest I'd ever heard. I listened to him on the radio all the time. And he was my friend Sharlene's older brother, so I knew a few additional facts about him than I might have otherwise.

Like that he was impulsive.

And loud.

And kind of a manwhore.

Then again, he had a rep in town, so most women knew these things, too. It was just that Shar had actually confirmed them for me.

Blake landed a decent punch and sent the other guy stumbling. But Dopey Dude got back up.

Oh, boy.

Shar was going to be *so* pissed when she heard about this. And she would. Probably within three minutes or less. Gossip traveled at the speed of sound in Mirabelle Harbor.

There was more yelling between the men, along with a bunch of shouts from the sports-bar crowd surrounding them. It reminded me of the stupid hall fights I'd had the misfortune to have to try to break up at the high school. Dumb boy behavior at its finest. Guys who fought each other because they couldn't rationally reason their way through a discussion. So foolish and immature. And, worse, so painful to the people who actually cared about these cretins.

Dopey Dude landed a crushing blow to Blake's abdomen. He doubled over and fell to the pavement. Then the other guy started to seriously pummel Blake while the crowd alternately jeered, taunted, and screamed their encouragement.

I winced. Blake's dark hair was matted against his forehead with sweat and, also, with some fresh blood. He had a gash across his cheekbones, dirt on his face and neck, and more blood dripping from the corner of his mouth.

And he was devastatingly handsome, even then.

Although, with the angry eyes and the snarl on his lips, he looked like the poster child for one the French revolutionary insurgents in *Les Misérables*. If he decided to build a barricade, storm the Bastille, or lead the crowd in the first verse of "Do You Hear the People Sing?" I wouldn't dare to stand in his way.

The fact that I couldn't guess whether he'd be more like a hero or a terrorist in any uprising made me immediately uncomfortable, though. I hadn't known he'd be like this. His sister could get a little fiery sometimes, but Shar had a marshmallow heart. Blake, by contrast, looked both self-destructive and vicious. Like he could quite effectively kill someone.

Finally, an officer came on the scene and broke up the fight. He ordered us all to leave, but I was rooted to the spot. I couldn't take my eyes off Blake's cut-up face. So many bruises, and he was even spitting blood.

Lisa nudged me. "Let's go, Vicky."

Before I could make my feet move, Blake looked up at me and our gazes collided. I kept imagining the shock Shar would feel if she saw her brother in this horribly battered, sweaty, and drunken state. She was very protective of her family. But nothing was going to protect Blake from the wrath of one massive hangover and the need for some serious first aid.

His eyes turned even darker and they narrowed dangerously as he continued to stare at me.

Christine tugged me away.

"They were like a couple of wasted jocks after a football game," she observed on the drive home.

"I know. I was thinking the same thing. Like those boys that get into fights in the school cafeteria. With them, it's all crazy levels of testosterone and impaired judgment, leading to damage of property and reckless endangerment of themselves and others. Imagine someone acting that way after being out of high school for fifteen years? It's like they never got all the way through adolescence."

Christine nodded. "Although I can't say being a mature grownup all the time is a barrel of laughs."

I smiled. "True. But anything is better than being forever seventeen."

I remembered myself at seventeen and suppressed a shudder. That was one time of my life I'd *never* want to relive, and I had daily witness as to why in my classroom.

Though, if forced to be completely honest with myself, one of the main reasons I'd been drawn to teaching was to see if I could make high school a better experience for kids like me. For those quirky, quiet, culture-loving, rule-following bookworms who really wanted to learn. Not that I was so different now, really. It was just that, back then, I'd felt so alone. I hadn't realized there might be others like me out there.

At least I had good female friends. But it was too bad my male counterpart didn't seem to exist. At least not in large enough quantities to keep searching for him. There were probably only fifty straight, single, American men who'd fit my criteria for dating. And chances were high that they were spread randomly across the United States. I'd be lucky to find even one or two anywhere in Illinois. My ideal, most compatible love match was probably living in a remote town in northern New Mexico or something.

I said goodnight to Christine, went inside my apartment, and leaned against the door with a deep sigh. I should go to sleep, but I just couldn't. All I'd be able to see behind my closed eyes would be Blake Michaelsen's bloodied, infuriated face.

So, instead, I made myself a cup of tea and greeted my cat Napoleon, who was in one of his antisocial moods. He peeked out from under the chair to brush my leg, and then he disappeared somewhere in my bedroom.

I took my Earl Grey into the living room and perused my DVD rack for a period drama that wasn't six or more hours long. That narrowed down my choices considerably.

But, as I selected a beloved two-hour adaptation of Jane Austen's *Persuasion* and settled into a comfy spot in the middle of my sofa, I had to face the facts: I'd already become one of "those" women. My chances of finding a man I'd consider to be even tolerable—let alone one I could actually live with—were about as likely as getting struck by lightning during a sandstorm.

On the African desert.

While I was doing shots of tequila with a handful of locals and the entire cast of the Broadway musical *Hamilton*...because we all just happened to be touring the Sahara together during Spring Break or something.

In other words, I'd be single for the rest of my life. The sooner I made peace with that truth, the better.

CHAPTER THREE

~*Vicky*~

"*Comment dit-on* 'How are you feeling today?' *en français*?" I asked my fourth period French III honors class on Tuesday. They loved playing the "How Do You Say" Q&A game with French phrases at the end of every period.

Stephanie's hand shot up like a rocket. "*Comment vous sentez-vous aujourd'hui*," she said with well-deserved confidence. That girl studied.

"*Absolument*," I replied. "*Et comment dit-on*...mmm, 'How old are you?' *en français*?"

"*Quel âge as-tu?*" Tyler responded.

"*Fantastique*." I paused. "Which train should I take to Paris?"

Amanda raised her hand. I nodded to her and she said, "*Quel train est le meilleur pour le voyage à Paris?*"

"*Très bien*," I said with a laugh. "That works, Amanda. It's a bit of a roundabout way of getting there, though. A slightly more direct phrase might be '*Quel train dois-je prendre à Paris?*' But what's important is that you've managed to convey the meaning of your question. Learning a foreign language is all about communicating, and there's not just one way to do that."

Now it was my turn. The kids could ask me how to say specific phrases in French, and they delighted in coming up with really funny and convoluted ones.

Carson said, "Mademoiselle Bernier, *comment dit-on,* 'Will you go to the Homecoming dance with me?'" Then he winked really obviously at Amanda, who blushed all the way up to her short and very blond roots.

"Veux-tu aller à la danse de Homecoming avec moi?" I said, unable to hide my grin. I'd had Amanda and Carson in my French classes since they were freshmen, and it had been so sweet to see the two of them bond and, eventually, start dating. "And what might the response be to such a question?" I asked the class.

Amanda looked too embarrassed to be called on, but Carson's friend Eddie clutched his heart and piped up, *"Oooh, Carson, mais oui! Tu es mon petit chou."*

The class erupted with laughter. It wasn't every day that one junior boy called another one "his little cabbage." *Mon petit chou,* however, was a traditional term of endearment in France, which was similar to saying "my little darling." It was fun to watch the kids embrace these cultural tidbits and make them their own.

"Okay, *merci beaucoup,* Eddie. Anyone else have another phrase?"

Stephanie wanted to know how to say "There's too much homework for this week in September."

I raised an eyebrow at her and she grinned.

"I think you all know that one," I told the class. "C'mon. Try to construct it."

"Il y a trop de devoirs pour cette semaine du Septembre," Janette tried.

"Very close," I said. "It would be *en Septembre.*" I nodded at her. *"Bien. Compris?"*

"Oui, Mademoiselle," she said.

Graham, another guy in the class and a good pal of Tyler's, said, *"Comment dit-on* 'I am a secret superhero and one of the Masters of the Universe.'" He fist-bumped the air comically and the whole class laughed again, just as the bell rang to end the period.

I rolled my eyes and said, *"Comment dit-on* 'Saved by the bell'?"

The students chorused, *"Sauvé par le gong!"* We'd used that phrase many times before. It was one of their favorites.

I smiled and clapped my hands, dismissing them. They were already my most beloved class, perhaps because I'd been fortunate to have gotten to know the individual students in it so well over the past few years. I was proud of them. They'd all come such a long way since freshmen year. I knew already that it was going to be hard to see them graduate when they were seniors.

My next class was less enthusiastic and, thus, not quite as fun to teach, but I was hoping this would improve before the end of the semester. In any case, I was always glad to have my lunch hour between fourth period and sixth, so I could shift gears.

Stephanie, however, came up to me after class and said, "I told the rest of committee to meet here. They all have fifth period lunch. Unless you'd rather go to the cafeteria, Mademoiselle."

For a second, I had no idea what she was talking about...then it came flooding back. "Oh, yes! Homecoming. Meeting in here is fine," I assured her.

When Stephanie had asked me to be the faculty advisor for the students' Homecoming committee at the end of May, I'd agreed without thinking twice. She was such a hardworker and overachiever that I knew everything would be well organized, and I was happy to supervise. But we'd been back at school for just over a week, and my head was full of other new school year details. I'd forgotten that today was the day of the first committee meeting.

"Who else is on the planning committee?" I asked her as we both pulled out our lunch sandwiches.

"Matt Rosatti, the junior class president," she recited dutifully. "Alexis Cho, the VP, and Heath Murray, who's doing the logo design for the posters and stuff."

I knew and liked all of these kids. Matt and Alexis were quite different from each other and had some individual struggles at various times during their high-school careers, but both were natural leaders. Heath was a shy junior, but he was supremely talented in art. I knew he'd do an excellent job with that task as well.

One at a time, the other three students trooped into the room. Matt had gotten a hot lunch from the cafeteria—it was cheeseburger day. Alexis just had a gigantic soda and a granola bar. And Heath brought in a bag lunch, which, as far as I could tell, consisted of the interesting meal combination of sushi and corn chips.

"Feel free to get started whenever you're all ready," I told the students. "I'm here if you need me, and I'm listening, but this is your event and I want you to run it however you'd feel best."

Stephanie nodded. "Thanks, Mademoiselle." She turned to the other kids and pulled out a sheet of notepaper. "I've got a list of things we need to decide on. Colors. Theme. Budget allocations for decorations, music, and food. And the cost of the tickets, particularly how many we need to sell in order to break even. Everyone should have gotten an email from me with an area to brainstorm, so maybe we can start by discussing each of those now." She glanced at the class president, and he nodded.

"Theme was my topic," Matt said. "I came up with a bunch of possibilities, but these are my three favorites. 'Chain Reaction'—like a science theme that focuses on the dynamics of attraction and magnetism."

Alexis rolled her eyes. "Is this really about

Homecoming, or are you just trying to put your AP Physics notes to good use?"

"It's not a crime to like science," he shot back, along with a teasing look that was more than a little menacing. "And it's original. I don't think any class before has used physics metaphors in their theme."

Stephanie squinted at him. And Heath, quiet as he was, slightly shook his head.

"Fine," Matt said. "I have other ideas. How about 'Fairy Tales Come True' then? *Cinderella. Sleeping Beauty. Aladdin.* Or whatever."

"That might be a big overdone," Stephanie said diplomatically.

"Which is a nice way of saying it's majorly lame," added Alexis.

Heath was more obvious in his head shaking this time.

Matt looked at me and shrugged. "Tough crowd."

I laughed. "They're very good suggestions, Matt, but I think you can strike a balance between too unusual and not quite unusual enough. What's your third idea?"

"Oh, 'Decades' was number three," he said.

"*All* decades?" Stephanie asked with a hint of concern.

"No," Matt said. "We'd narrow it down to one and focus our theme around that. 'Swinging '40s' or 'Psychedelic '60s' or 'Totally Rad '80s' or whichever other one we want. We could decorate to match the era."

"I could actually go with that," Alexis said.

Heath, who hadn't taken his eyes off the pretty and outspoken Vice President since he entered the room, was quick to agree with Alexis.

Stephanie consulted her notes carefully and nodded. "I like it." Then she looked at me. "Any objections to Matt's 'Decades' idea, Mademoiselle?"

"None at all," I said. "That sounds fun."

"Heath," Stephanie said, "didn't you already design something with a Seventies theme?"

31

"Yeah. In junior high," he mumbled.

"Oh, that's right! The mock Watergate trials we did in social studies," Alexis said. "Those backdrops were great."

Heath's face lit up as he smiled his thanks at her, but he seemed rendered speechless by her praise. Wow. The boy had it bad.

Alexis, however, didn't seem to realize the effect she had on him. "I think the Eighties would be a cool decade. Our class hasn't done anything with that, and the music is fun to dance to and sort of familiar. The Forties would be classy and all, but no one would know the songs."

"I know *some* of the songs," Matt said, probably just to be contrary and to tease Alexis. "Not *everyone* in our class is ignorant of pop culture from prior eras just because—"

"Oh, stop!" Alexis threw her granola bar wrapper at him and he laughed.

Stephanie tried to rein them in. "So, Eighties will be our decade then?"

All agreed.

"Great. Moving on to colors..." she said.

After some debate, the kids chose black and purple. They also made a decision on ticket prices, based on last year's profits, and hashed out a basic budget for what they'd projected decorating and entertainment costs would be.

Alexis had been in charge of collecting ideas for the music during the dance. "A live band is too expensive," she said, "and hiring someone to spin records who isn't a professional is risky. Remember what happened to my brother's prom when they did that two years ago?"

There were groans and nods from the other kids. I hadn't chaperoned that dance, but I'd heard from the other teachers and the kids that it had been pretty bad.

"So, I think we want a professional DJ, and last year's committee chose someone from 102.5," Alexis continued. "They're local, they might give us a break on the price, and they've done a lot of events."

I couldn't hear 102.5 mentioned without thinking about Shar's brother. I imagined he wasn't in very good shape this morning. I wouldn't have been if I'd looked like that at the end of the night. But who knew with him? Maybe he had such a high tolerance for alcohol that he recovered quicker than most.

"Didn't Amelia Lockett spin tunes last year?" Matt asked. "Let's have her do it again. She's hot."

Heath cracked a smile and Stephanie nodded thoughtfully, but Alexis said, "I think Blake Michaelsen would be perfect."

Oh, my God. No.

"Why?" Matt asked.

Yeah, why? I asked Alexis in my head.

"Because he's funny. Even more in person than on the radio," she said. "I saw him host a dance off in Eastman Field a few summers ago, and he was hilarious."

He hosted a dance off?

My throat was making a squeaky, protesting sound, but it was too soft for the VP to hear.

Stephanie jumped in and said, "I like Blake, too. His sister, Ms. Boyd, was my favorite teacher in junior high, and he came into her English class once to give us a talk on radio and communications. He was really good."

He gave talks to Shar's students? She'd never told me that.

"And he's really cute," Alexis added with a snotty look in Matt's direction.

Heath's brow crinkled. Ah. That was an observation he didn't like.

I finally found my voice so I could jump in. "Well, I feel it's important to point out, as your advisor, that you're going to want to make sure to choose someone you can rely on and work well with. Blake has a very, um, distinctive personality. But Amelia has more recent experience DJ'ing the dance. So, perhaps, it'd be a bit easier to plan the event with her, being that she's more familiar with Homecoming specifically."

Stephanie nodded at me. "We could take a vote," she suggested. "Blake or Amelia. And Mademoiselle Bernier could be our tie breaker."

I grinned at her. "That sounds fair."

More truthfully, it would at least *seem* fair, but the outcome would turn out exactly as I wanted. The guys would vote for Amelia. The girls would vote for Blake. And then I'd choose Amelia to break the tie and to keep my blood pressure at normal levels. All would be well.

"Okay," Alexis said. "I vote for Blake."

"Amelia, hands down," Matt stated.

"Blake," Stephanie said.

All eyes turned toward Heath. But his eyes turned toward Alexis, and I immediately realized the error of my assumptions.

Oh, damn.

"Blake," Heath said.

"Yes!" squealed the girls.

"Aw, man! Why d'ya pick him?" Matt asked.

Heath shrugged. "'Cuz he's cool." That was what he said aloud anyway. What his body language conveyed, however, was *Whatever Alexis wants, I want.*

And, so, it was three to one. I didn't even get a chance to vote.

Merde.

I'd have to work with him on this event. Sexy but oh-so-irresponsible Blake Michaelsen. What a way to start the new school year...

The kids ran through some tentative ideas for the Homecoming Week schedule, but I'd stopped actively listening.

Alexis called the radio station and left a message for Blake.

Stephanie made check marks next to just about every item on her agenda.

Matt recovered his good humor quickly by brainstorming a bunch of Eighties fads that they could incorporate into the week of activities.

And Heath was still beaming from the grin Alexis had given him after he'd voted on her side, along with an offer from her to help him this weekend as he sifted through images for logo ideas. The kid looked like he was flying through the air as if on a levitating (à la *Back to the Future*) skateboard when the two of them walked out of the classroom together.

Well, at least *someone* was having a good day. My week was getting worse by the second. And now I'd not only have to be present at the next meeting on Thursday, but if Blake accepted the job, he'd be there, too.

I sincerely hoped he'd behave himself. Or at least try to refrain from slugging anybody.

CHAPTER FOUR

~*Blake*~

*O*h. *My. Effing. God.*

My head was filled with those little cotton balls that they used at the doctor's office to swipe an injection site before giving a shot. Everything was fuzzy. Except when it was not. Because, unfortunately, my head also seemed to be filled with a handful of loose razor blades that felt a helluva lot like they were slicing up bits of my brain when there was the slightest sound.

So when the phone rang, it was like shrapnel exploding in my cranium, paired with the sound of a cannon ball going off in stereo in both my ears.

I reached for the phone, just to make it stop. "Wha—" I said.

"Blake?" a voice I recognized as one of my bosses said. But *which* boss?

"Mmm?" I managed.

The man cleared his throat. "I'm sorry. Did I wake you?" he asked, incredulous.

I glanced at the time. 11:46. Not bad. It was still

technically morning.

"No, no. I just had a headache, so I was resting." Totally true, at least that first part of the sentence. I gripped my forehead like a vise, trying to keep my brains from spilling out of my skull. "What can I do for you, uh...Leonard?" I said, hoping I'd guessed right on the name.

"We got a call on the main line just a few minutes ago from the high school. It was a message for you. A bunch of kids with the Homecoming committee were hoping you might be available to DJ the dance in a few weeks. Said they had a meeting this Thursday afternoon and were hoping you could be there to talk over the details with them." He paused. "I know Thursday is one of your longer days at the station, so I wanted to give you a heads up so you could check your schedule about that afternoon and about the dance on Friday, October second."

"High schoolers," I murmured. "Homecoming dance..." My head felt like it was going to implode. I could only repeat key phrases in hopes that something would sink in. "This Thursday and October second?"

"Yeah," Leonard said. "What's your schedule like? Can you do them?"

I would've laughed if it didn't hurt so much. My "schedule" for this week revolved entirely around just showing up to my job and managing to stay upright. Ambition at its finest. And I hadn't given a single thought to what I was doing next month. But I said, "Let me just check my calendar." Then I paused, appreciating the momentary silence and rubbing my temples with both hands. Finally, I picked up my phone again. "Both of those dates look open right now."

"Great!" he said. "I'll call the kids back and let them know that you and 102.5 are officially on board for Homecoming."

"Excellent. See you...later," I muttered. Hopefully *much*

later. I clicked off, collapsed onto my pillow, and moaned, but no one came to my rescue.

Aw, that wasn't strictly true. Winston bounded over to me, licking my face. Then he dashed to the front door, scratched on it, and barked a couple of times.

Yeah, I didn't doubt he needed to go out. So, for his sake, I dragged my hung-over body out of bed and forced myself to start the day.

One of the perks of working for a radio station was that it wasn't a nine-to-five kind of job. There was some built-in variety.

I worked almost every day of the week, but some days I was only on the air for a couple of hours, and then I did paperwork or answered phone calls. Other days it might be a straight six-hour shift or a split shift with two- or three-hour rotations—one morning, one night—along with an outside event, like a party. Because we were a small crew at a privately owned station, we covered for each other and took turns doing late nights, weekends, and out-of-town gigs. It helped to keep the routine from settling in my bones and boring the hell out of me.

So, after a long on-air rotation on Thursday, I was still technically on the clock when I arrived at Mirabelle Harbor High School around 3:15 p.m. and was greeted at the office by a chatty member of the Homecoming committee. Alexis something or other. She escorted me to the meeting location.

Whoa. And there was the French teacher babe, pacing in the middle of her classroom.

Gotta love "community outreach" and the surprises it could bring. I had a fresh appreciation for the variety of my job. Spice. Of. Life.

I removed my baseball cap and slid off my sunglasses when the babe—Vicky—looked my way.

"Hey, there," I said, extending my hand to her.

She looked at me suspiciously, like I might be holding a grenade or something. So I twisted my hand a bit, so she could see my open palm. Her smile seemed forced as she reached out to grasp it.

Small hands. Soft skin. So feminine. I reluctantly let go as she pulled away. She seemed a little off kilter, still staring strangely at me. I sent her my most charming smile.

She took a literal step back, cleared her throat, and said stiffly, "Hello, Mr. Michaelsen. I'm Vicky Bernier, staff advisor to the Homecoming committee."

Very formal and controlled. Hmm, that was no fun. I wanted to throw her off balance again because she was cute when she was flustered and, hey, I was that kind of guy.

So I beamed an even bigger grin at her. "And you're a friend of my sister's," I said, curious to see if that would disarm her or make her more concerned.

From the expression on her face, definitely the latter. Huh.

"Yes," she said slowly. "I've heard a lot about you from Shar."

Damn. What did my sister tell her to make her scowl at me like that? Couldn't be good.

But I said, "Praising my awesomeness, no doubt, right?"

She didn't deign to reply, which was a bad sign. I'd have to have a little chat with Shar later.

I turned my attention to the four teenagers in the classroom who were gaping at us like we were cast members on some reality TV dating show.

The chatty girl who'd met me at the office was the first to speak. "On behalf of the Homecoming committee, we're all so glad you could meet with us today, Mr. Michaelsen. And we're super psyched that you'll be DJ'ing our dance."

One of the two guys, who turned out to be the junior class president, looked a little less enthusiastic than the rest, but all the kids cheered.

"It's gonna be so great, Mr. Michaelsen," another girl who introduced herself as Stephanie Little said.

I grinned at her. "Call me Blake. All of you. Please." I glanced over at the French teacher as I said this. She was as impassive as granite. "And thanks for the warm welcome, everyone. I promise we'll make this more fun than a Roman orgy."

The class president's eyes brightened about as much as the French teacher's darkened when I said those words. Kinda high strung, wasn't she? I had a memory flash of Vicky outside the bars on Monday night with that same disapproving expression on her pretty face. She might have the body of a hottie, but her attitude was a real chiller. Too bad.

Chatty Girl/Alexis said, "We wanted to share with you our plans for the week and some of the details we've worked out so far, just to make sure the music at the dance would reflect our theme."

"Yeah, shoot," I said, sitting down in one of the student desks. That brought back such an unwelcome wave of recollection about being in high school that I stood back up and leaned against the desk instead. I'd felt so damn trapped in this building when I was a teenager. Kind of eerie to be back here. Even for a half hour.

Stephanie said, "I've got the tentative schedule right here." She handed Alexis a sheet of paper, but all the kids seemed well versed on the upcoming events, which involved window painting and school spirit days.

Matt, the class president, said, "We're planning to have a car wash Sunday afternoon the twenty-seventh to kick off Homecoming Week and to raise extra money for refreshments for the Friday night dance."

"It'll be an Eighties theme," Stephanie explained, "so

we'd love a bunch of music from that era."

"Sure," I said.

"And the car wash will probably be during your shift at the radio station," Alexis added. "We'll be playing 102.5 all afternoon while we work."

I nodded. "Sounds cool. How about I give you kids a shout out on the air. Would that help? Tell the listeners to come down to the high school for a car wash because you all need to make money to, uh...pay for the beer you're bringing into the dance."

Matt laughed and even the quiet guy of the group— Heath—cracked a smile. Mademoiselle Frenchie did not.

"Mr. Michaelsen—" Vicky began.

"Blake," I reminded her.

"Blake," she repeated. "I know you're just joking around, of course, but you really can't say things like—"

"Oh, relax," I interrupted. "I'm sure the kids were aware that I was completely kidding. Right?"

"Right," they all chorused.

"Because everyone knows it's a *lot* harder to sneak beer into a dance than it is to bring in hard liquor," I continued with a straight face, just to needle her. I turned to the teens. "My advice is to go right for the vodka. It's clear and nearly odorless. It can pass for water, unless someone tastes it."

Matt laughed so hard he literally fell out of his desk chair. He fist-bumped me from the floor. The other kids were laughing, too. Vicky remained *very* unamused. I'd have to tell Shar what an uptight stick-in-the-mud her friend was.

"You were totally right about this guy," Matt said to Alexis. Then, to me, "You're awesome, man."

I shrugged with faux modesty. "That's what I've been told."

The French teacher crossed her arms. "Blake, I've already said—"

41

"Oh, c'mon," I cajoled. "You're telling me you *never* snuck a flask of an alcoholic beverage into an event when you were in high school? You know, some night after a big game when you met your friends under the bleachers. When you grabbed a few swigs of something to, like, loosen up a little, so you could work up the courage to kiss that person you'd been scoping out in math class all semester. When you maybe found a dark corner of the gym during the dance and ran your fingers down—"

"No!" she insisted, although I saw the color rushing to her cheeks, heating them. I would've paid hard cash to know what memories my comments dredged up in her mind.

The teens couldn't have been more riveted if this had been the final episode of *The*-freakin'-*Bachelor*, complete with roses and a fantasy suite and filmed right in front of them. I had to admit, it cheered me up to see Vicky look so uncomfortable. If she was going to act like I was an immature, terrible influence then, hell, I could play the part better than she could ever imagine. I was *born* to be a bad boy. And someone needed to get this chick to lighten the fuck up. Guess that job was gonna fall to me.

I didn't let her launch into a lecture. I just swung back to the kids and told them, "Count on me to give you a shout out during the car wash on September twenty-seventh, and I'll also make up a list of Eighties tunes that I can spin at the dance. About two-and-a-half to three hours worth of songs, if I'm right, yes?"

Stephanie nodded.

"Good. I can show them to you all beforehand, so you can let me know if you want any others added or some of them nixed."

"That's so great!" Stephanie piped up. "It'd be wonderful to have an idea of the playlist by our next meeting."

Not to be outdone in the enthusiasm department, Alexis

said, "Could you, maybe, email it to one of us before our meeting next Thursday? Would that be enough time for you?"

"Sure," I said.

"You can send it to me," Alexis offered.

"Or me," Stephanie volunteered.

The girls were adorable—they'd grow up to be heartbreakers someday—but it was their teacher who kept snagging my attention, and she clearly didn't appreciate my having any private interactions with her students.

"As the advisor," Vicky stated firmly, "I'll give you my school email address, and you can send it to *me*. I'll read through the song list and pass it on to the committee."

Ah. So she was going to play the role of the censor. That wouldn't do. At all.

"You all meet next Thursday?" I asked. "Like now? Same time, same location?"

"Yep," Matt said.

"Well, why don't I just drop off the list in person then? That way, if there are any objections to the songs on the playlist—" I sent Vicky a pointed glance. "We can discuss it as a group."

"Oh, you don't have to take time out of your day again—" the French teacher began.

"Yes!" Stephanie and Alexis said together.

"Sounds great!" Matt added.

Heath smiled at me.

I couldn't hide a small grin of triumph as the teens summarily outvoted their teacher. "There are some bad-ass lost Eighties hits," I whispered conspiratorially to the kids.

"Like the extended version of Tone Lōc's 'Funky Cold Medina'?" Matt suggested.

"Oh, you like that one, do you?" I said with a laugh. "Okay. Let me see what I can dig up for you guys that might be fun and just a little lewd. Gotta keep those chaperones on their toes. We don't want them falling asleep, and a couple hours of Journey ballads might just do that to 'em."

I nodded at Matt, who gave me a thumbs up.

Vicky opened her mouth to voice yet another objection, but I cut her off.

"Relax, Mademoiselle. It'll be a clean program...mostly. Don't lose your sense of humor."

I caught a glint in her eye that I wasn't sure how to interpret, but I could almost see the wheels in her gorgeous head spinning. I decided it'd be better if I directed the course of the rest of the discussion.

"Since you're the advisor and all," I said, "I take it you're going to be there during the dance?"

She exhaled and narrowed her eyes at me. "Of course I'll be there, Blake. And I'll make sure *everyone* behaves themselves and has fun."

"Two oxymoronic ideas if I've ever heard them, but whatever you say." Then I addressed the kids again. "I've just got one piece of advice for you all. If you can't be *really* good, at least be bad in a *really* interesting way."

And with those words and a parting wave to the teens, I said goodbye. To Vicky in particular, I sent a special little wink and added, "Catch you next week, Mademoiselle."

My guess was that, if I'd given her even half a second to respond, the teacher would've said (in English or in French) something like, "Not if I catch sight of you first."

But I slipped through the door quickly, out of the high school, and back to the Land of the Free.

Damn. I might not be a shining example of adulthood, but I'd never been happier to be over twenty-one and out from under the thumb of authority.

Even if that authority came in the form of a foxy French-speaking babe who had lips like a cherry pop and tits that were so tempting it was going to take some serious effort not to reach out and touch her.

Aw, what was I saying?

It would probably take *too much* effort. And, as plenty of people loved to point out, self control had never been my strong suit anyway.

So, I'd just have to figure out a way to seduce her. With a little time, a little charm, and a little luck...I think I could get her to like me.

CHAPTER FIVE

~*Vicky*~

"I absolutely cannot stand him," I said aloud. "He's immature, unromantic, and inappropriate. He can barely suppress his vulgar impulses. He's a bad role model for teens. And he's far worse to deal with than any high-school kid I've ever met. And I've been teaching for eleven years!"

My companion just stared at me, occasionally blinking but not uttering a sound.

"He was in my classroom for what? Twenty minutes yesterday afternoon? Twenty-five tops? And he talked nonstop for most of it. Maybe I'm just being idealistic here, but I don't think the kids would even think to behave poorly without a bad influence like that. He was actively encouraging them to bring liquor to a school event, grope each other under the bleachers and at the dance, disrespect authority, and perpetuate the stereotype that kids and chaperones had to be at odds."

I paused, realizing that the latter was what pissed me off the most. I'd worked hard for years to develop a strong and respectful relationship with my students, and Blake Michaelsen had created a wedge between them and me in less than a half hour. Setting me up to be some kind of "enemy of the youth" or something, just because I wanted Homecoming Week to run smoothly and legally. The bastard.

"And now I'll have to keep an eye on *him* at the dance, even more than the kids," I added, "because if things spiral out of control at Blake's urging, it'll reflect poorly not only on me but, also, on the other staff members and parents who've agreed to chaperone."

My companion made an odd sound. Sort of like a yawn.

"C'mon, Napoleon. I know you know what this means to me. I *care* about my students, and I'm hopeful they'll grow up to be kind adults who have happy memories of high school. But Homecoming, with Blake involved, is going to be *un cauchemar*—a nightmare. He's turning the dance from a sweet high-school romantic comedy into a rowdy teen party movie. It's like the difference between *The Princess Diaries* and *American Pie*."

My cat had apparently listened to my ranting long enough or had no interest in my pop-culture references because he got up from the sofa, went for a stroll around my apartment, and eventually headed to the kitchen for a snack from his food bowl. So much for my most trusted confidante.

Normally, I'd confide my school-related woes to one of my foreign-language department friends or to other teacher pals like Shar or Julia.

But, for obvious reasons, I didn't feel comfortable whining to Shar about her big brother. Family ties had a tensile strength like platinum when it came to the Michaelsen clan.

And Julia hadn't been around much lately. She was caught up in a whirlwind of change in her life, and I didn't want to add any drama to it. As it was, she had a fairy-tale romance in progress, and I didn't begrudge her that for a second. She'd had to walk through a trail of heartbreak first to get there.

But I had to admit that I envied her love story. Both of them really—the one she'd had with her late husband and the new one that was just developing. I'd been in several long-term relationships, but none of them had turned out a fraction as well. I'd never had a fling or a one-night stand. I kept trying to hold out for true love—like the kind my parents had—but it hadn't worked out the same for me.

I glanced at the wall, which had a framed picture of my mom and dad. They'd been college sweethearts, who'd been happily married for thirty-seven years now. It had been a little daunting to watch them and to always wonder, "Will I ever have a romance like that?"

Short answer: Not likely.

But it warmed my heart to see students like Heath falling for Alexis, or Carson's blossoming love story with Amanda, and to know that their burgeoning young romances were promising ones. That, even if their relationships didn't last beyond high school, these kids might just get a taste of that sweet young love fairy tale.

But a guy like Blake had a talent for leaching away the sweetness and innocence of first love. He made a romantic dance all about alcohol and sex against the wall and raunchy lyrics and bad-boy behavior. Small-minded, infantile guys like him, who still acted like the worst type of adolescents weren't high on my list of people to associate with. Period. Didn't matter how sexy his voice was. Or how hot his body.

I loved the men of romance novels and movies where the hero was not only dashing but moral. Men of high principles in the past or in the present. Chivalry and honorable behavior from any era turned me on, even more than six-pack abs and witty comebacks. If a man could be kind, clever, cute, *and* genuine, I'd fall at his feet.

But I wasn't finding such a man...at least not outside of films and novels.

And I respected true romance too much to be willing to compromise love's integrity by settling for anything less.

I finally dragged myself away from the sofa and decided it was high time to go grocery shopping, or I'd be eating peanut butter and jelly sandwiches all weekend.

Friday night at Mirabelle Market was a quiet place.

No, that was a massive understatement. It was like going to the community swimming pool at the end of summer, once school was back in session. Anyone in town who had the remotest social life wasn't buying fresh produce at 8:23 p.m. on a weekend night.

So, of course, the only person I ran into at the store was somebody from the singles' group.

"Hi, Bill," I said, waving to the tall, balding man.

"Vicky! Good to see you," he said kindly. "How are the new students this year?"

Bill Dennon was in his late thirties, divorced, a former prosecuting attorney ("a recovering lawyer," he often joked), and a good guy. Sadly, he wasn't my type, but I always enjoyed chatting with him.

"The kids are great," I told him, and I meant that, although thinking about Blake Michaelsen and the Homecoming frustrations made me scowl.

"You sure about that?" Bill said with a laugh. "Maybe I should be reading into what you *didn't* say. 'The kids are great...but the administrators suck.' Something like that?"

I burst out laughing. "Definitely something like that. The adults are almost always harder to deal with than the students."

"You need to have some fun and get away from it all," he said. "I'm glad you're around this weekend. You'll be coming out with the group tomorrow night, right?"

"Um..." I picked up a random mango from the bin next to us and began examining it, to buy a little time. I'd put the next Quest group outing on my calendar a couple of weeks ago—we were all planning to meet for dinner at Drew's Diner in downtown Mirabelle Harbor—but that was before this whole Homecoming thing started. Shar rarely missed a Quest gathering, which meant she'd be there. And I'd have to avoid her inevitable questions. "I don't know, Bill," I said finally. "It's been a long week—"

"It was just four days," he protested. "Although those weeks can seem like the longest. Trying to cram five days of work into only four."

"Exactly."

"All the more reason to come out with us. Just to relax and catch up with friends. There are plenty of other nights left to stay home alone and watch TV." He smiled as he said this, but there was a ribbon of sadness and loneliness beneath the words. I recognized those emotions all too well.

"That's true," I admitted. "I'm still tempted to stay in and read all night," which was my favorite pastime when I was finished with grading and lesson plans. "But I'll think about it."

"Good," he said. "It's not the same without your bright smile, Vicky."

"Aw, Bill, thank you." How did he know I needed to hear some kind words tonight? I gave him a quick hug, and he left me to my mango selection as he headed off to finish his own shopping.

By the time I got home and unloaded my groceries, though, I was even more convinced that staying home tomorrow would be the better option. Sweet as Bill and the other Quest members were, I'd downloaded a new Jane Austen fan fiction story to my ebook reader, and it had been calling me all week.

But anyone who thought I'd get off the hook that easily, clearly hadn't met Sharlene Michaelsen Boyd.

"What do you mean you're not coming?" Shar texted

me the next afternoon when I replied to her message about the event. "OF COURSE you're coming. I can pick you up."

Shar and I lived only a couple of blocks apart. I was in an apartment complex near Bangkok Gardens and she was in the condo unit just west and south of me, further down Crescent Lane. It was not out of character for her to show up at my door either and insist on dragging me somewhere.

"It's okay," I texted back, relenting. "I'll go tonight, but I'll meet you there. I have some errands to run first."

This wasn't entirely the truth (I'd already run my errands), but it was safer not to be trapped in a vehicle with Shar if she got into one of her question-asking moods.

When I arrived at Drew's Diner that night, more than half the Quest group was already there, Shar included. She waved me over to a section at the right, by the windows, where several tables had been pushed together and pitchers of lemonade and margaritas had already been ordered.

"Hey, great to see you here," she said, giving me a welcome hug and pointing to an open chair across the table from her. "Get all your errands done?"

"Erm...yep," I said.

"Excellent. That means you can stay out late with us," Shar concluded. "I haven't seen you since the school year started. How's it been going for you?"

"Good, good," I said, pausing to say hi to a new batch of people that just arrived and trying to gauge Shar's nonverbal cues. I was torn. I didn't want to bring up Blake and invite that kind of awkwardness into our conversation unnecessarily. But if she didn't know about my having met her brother, it would be a weird thing not to tell her. When she found out we'd been working together, she'd wonder why I didn't mention it.

Based on her good-natured grin and the lack of intensity on her face, I got the sense that she didn't know anything about Homecoming yet, though, which was interesting. It meant Blake hadn't said anything to her either.

"What's with the funny look?" Shar said with a laugh.

"Nothing, I just was going to ask if, um—" I was debating whether to say something about Blake or inquire after the start of her new English classes at the junior high, when there was a squeal. Elsie, one of the Quest members, jumped up from her place down the table and waved frantically at someone near the door. "Julia!"

Shar swiveled around with a grin, and everyone at the table looked over at Julia Crane as she skipped over to us.

Shar beamed at her. "You came!" And I realized that I wasn't the only one Shar had been badgering to come out tonight. "Glad to see you, girlfriend."

"You, too," Julia said with a wink at her BFF.

Julia and I waved at each other as Elsie pulled another chair over and made her sit down near the head of the table.

"Tell us *everything,*" Elsie insisted. "How was California? How is Dane doing? Will you be going back to see him anytime soon? Don't keep us in suspense!"

Julia laughed and graciously accepted the rapt attention of the Quest group members, but she and I had talked on several occasions, and I knew she was a private person. One who had experienced the unexpected death of her husband last year and who was now dealing with the semi-surreal challenge of navigating a new romance with a popular movie actor. The world wasn't inclined to give someone in that position much privacy.

"The California trip was...incredible," Julia said with a smile that infused her whole face with joy. "Dane was wonderful. Analise couldn't have had a better time at the movie studio and the sites around L.A. So, if my daughter has anything to say about it, we'll be flying out there every month."

Elsie looked gleeful. "And you?"

Another woman at the table named Therese said, "Tell

us about the man!"

It was a one-in-a-million love story that made my heart pound just thinking about it. Julia met her teen idol, Dane Tyler, twenty years after she'd fallen in love with him on the Silver Screen...and was now dating him for real.

Even if I met my British Dream Man someday (and, miraculously, he was straight), it wasn't as though it would be likely that something similar would happen to *me*. Normal life for normal people just didn't work like that.

Julia tried to satisfy the group's curiosity by telling a few stories about things she and her ten-year-old daughter did with Dane. However, I couldn't help but notice that, despite the blushes and the tone of secrecy, Julia didn't tell the Quest group anything that they couldn't have read in the tabloids or online. Shar, of course, by her noticeable *lack* of questioning, obviously knew the uncensored details. My guess was there were quite a few behind-the-scenes stories that the readers of the *Tinseltown Buzz* would have loved to have heard...

Me, too, for that matter. Although I could appreciate Julia's need for discretion.

When I finally got a few moments to speak to her alone in the powder room, I figured she'd had enough of people trying to pry, so I only congratulated her on her promising relationship.

"Thank you so much, Vicky," she said warmly. "It means a lot to me when someone is genuinely happy for us. I have to admit, that's not always the case." She didn't say this bitterly, but I could tell that—as much as the romance with Dane Tyler agreed with her—the media attention had worn her out.

"Is the press still being really intrusive?" I asked.

"Always," she said with a chuckle. "But Dane's worth it. He really took me by surprise. Guess Jane Austen was right about first impressions not necessarily being accurate."

We shared a laugh over that. Julia was a junior high English teacher, so she and I had a mutual love for Mr. Darcy in *Pride and Prejudice*. Although, if I were being honest, I was definitely the more fanatical of the two of us.

"Now, please, tell me about you," she said. "Everyone's always asking about me, but I miss hearing other news."

I thought of skirting what was really happening or saying something superficial, but Julia was sincere and I could really use her perspective.

"I'm okay. Mostly. I have a situation, though... How well do you know Shar's brother Blake?"

Her dark-blond eyebrows shot up. "A fair bit. But why? Has he done anyth—"

"No, no. It's not what you think. He's DJ'ing the Homecoming dance and I'm the committee advisor, which means we need to work together for the next few weeks, but I can't get a clear read on him."

Julia paused for a long moment, considering my words or, perhaps, how much to share with me. Finally, she said, "Hanging around Dane, I've learned a little about actors. I can tell you this about Blake—he has a veneer. I'm not sure when it started or why, but it's been there for as long as I've known him, and I think he hides behind it. Even, perhaps, with his family sometimes."

I took in this insight, surprised but grateful. It was an interesting observation on her part and, even though I didn't know Blake as well as Julia did, her perspective seemed to ring true. Not that it made me like the guy much better, but at least it didn't deepen my dislike.

"So you believe that, despite all his talking, he's pretty guarded?" I asked.

She nodded. "He has a gift for appearing open without actually giving anything away. Shar's complained about his cageyness many times. And I have no idea what it would take to get him to let someone in on his real feelings."

Julia certainly had more past interactions with the

Michaelsens than I did, but that wasn't always enough. After all, I'd *thought* I knew my ex-boyfriend Philippe and his family rather well, but I was still blindsided by his behavior. So familiarity was no guarantee of understanding somebody.

I knew this even as Julia was quick to reassure me that she was sure Blake had a good heart underneath it all. "Even if he seems reckless, I don't think he'd ever do anything truly bad," she said.

Once upon a time, I'd been more optimistic about people. In college, for instance, I'd dated the usual collection of guys that a future foreign-language teacher would be drawn to: European exchange students, other cultural junkies, international studies majors, one guy from Bogota, Colombia (until I found out he had a penchant for running drugs), and, of course, guys who'd studied French because it was considered a "language of love" and they thought it might help them get laid.

Philippe, whom I'd dated during my first few years of teaching, was a native French speaker but, in many ways, he'd fallen squarely into that later category. I just hadn't realized it at first. I'd been taken in by his charm and his projection of sincerity. It was only after we broke up that I could see he was a *seducer* not a romantic. Not even close to the same thing.

I thanked Julia for sharing her thoughts with me, and I let her mingle more with the other members of the Quest group. So many of them were anxious to talk with her, and they were nice people. Not only Bill and Shar, but Elsie, Therese, Alex, Martha, Linda, and Colleen. I couldn't help but wonder, though, why I was here. I'd come to enough gatherings by now to know that I wasn't going to find my soulmate in this group, much as I liked everyone on a personal level. I should have trusted my gut and just stayed home to read that story I was—

"You look like you're in another galaxy, a few million

light years away," Shar observed.

I smiled at her. "You caught me, although maybe just a mile or two away. At my apartment. On the sofa. With a good book." I shook my head and lowered my voice so only she could hear. "These get-togethers only remind me of dates from my past and why I'm still single. I'm feeling so old tonight."

"Don't say that. You're only two years older than me, and I refuse to throw in the towel just yet."

Shar was very fit, fast-moving, and sprite-like. I had a hard time imagining that she'd ever feel old. She certainly wouldn't look it for a long, long time. I told her this.

She shrugged me off. "I feel old and frustrated all the time, Vicky. But then I look at Julia and at my brothers Chance and Derek, and I see how much happier they all are now that they've met someone special. It gives me hope that true love exists out there."

True love was the golden ticket. The prize of a lifetime. The holy grail of fantasies. Who didn't want true love? But there was no magic spell to cast. No way to make it appear on command.

I murmured something noncommittal to Shar.

She crossed her arms and stared at me. "Okay, Vicky. There's something going on with you. Are you gonna tell me or what?"

I briefly considered the "or what" option, but I didn't want to worry a friend, and my cowardice was getting ridiculous.

"I, um...met your brother Blake on Thursday," I said, working hard to keep my tone neutral. "He's going to be DJ'ing the Homecoming dance. Did he mention that to you?"

Shar put her hands on her hips and shook her head. "But I know my brother. I love him but he's a pain. What did the asshat say to piss you off?"

"Oh, well, it wasn't...I mean, there wasn't a specific—"

I paused. Blake Michaelsen might not be my favorite person in the world, but Shar already looked very irritated, and I wasn't trying to turn his sister against him.

"So, it wasn't just *one* thing, eh?" Shar concluded grimly. "Can't say I'm surprised. He's been on a tear all month. It's a wonder the numbskull even has time to do his job in between getting into bar fights and oversleeping."

Ah. So she'd heard about the fight at Max's on Monday night. Not that I was shocked. She'd probably already chewed him out for that.

"And he completely missed a family gathering last night," she continued ranting, "claiming to be 'too tired.' What bullshit. More like 'too hung over.' Again. I'm tempted to march over to his place right now and—"

"Oh, please don't. At least not on my account. Meeting him wasn't that bad, Shar. It's just, he has a way of riling up the kids. They don't need a lot of encouragement to go wild, so..."

"I'm sorry, Vicky. I know he can act worse than a squirrelly teenager. I'll tell him to knock it off when he's with you."

"No, I don't want to get in between you, but I just wanted to ask—has he had a self-destructive bent for a long time?"

Shar pulled me away from the rest of the group so we could talk privately.

"He's always been a lover *and* a fighter, Vicky. His natural inclination is to kiss a woman he finds attractive, and then deal with the consequences afterward. Or to punch out a guy who's bothering him first, and ask questions later. He was the kid most likely to end up with stitches on the playground. The teen that the principal or deans immediately called to the office when there was a mysterious problem. But aside from some binge drinking at parties in high school or college, I've never known Blake to be out of control with alcohol—at least not until fairly recently. Chandler was always the family party animal. So different from his twin."

We shared a brief chuckle over that. Chandler's twin Chance was such a health nut that he rarely drank anything but bottled water.

"The thing is," Shar continued, "I know Blake's been drinking alone more often lately. As a kind of numbing tactic. And that, of course, worries me."

She had a haunted look on her face when she spoke about this, and I could tell it pained her to have to admit these things about her big brother. It was clear how much Shar loved every member of her family with her whole heart, but she wasn't one to see them idealistically. And if I'd been worried about her being offended by my lack of rapport with Blake, it was unnecessary.

She leaned in and said, "Just so you know, my brother loves to push other people's buttons. Don't let him bully you. He lives for that. And you have my permission to slap him if he makes any kind of a pass at you. I already know he thinks you're hot, so if he gets grabby—"

"WHAT?"

She laughed. "Yeah. He saw you at the radio station during the Dane Tyler reception this summer. He called you The Babe," she added with a grin.

This was news to me, and my shock must have shown.

Shar patted me gently on my arm. "Blake has the romantic attention span of a gnat, so just stand your ground and don't take his behavior personally. I keep hoping he'll grow up one day and behave like a gentleman. But that might take another decade or two." She sighed. "So, be forewarned."

CHAPTER SIX

~*Blake*~

There must be some law of quantum physics or something that stated that even if you've lived for years in the same town as someone and rarely laid eyes on that person before, once you've been officially introduced, you suddenly start seeing them freakin' everywhere.

After my little chat with the uptight Mademoiselle on Thursday, I hadn't expected to see her again so soon. Like at Mirabelle Market on Friday night.

The place was as dead as road kill. Maybe five people in the entire grocery store. And I was *this close* to walking up to Vicky and giving her a hard time in the produce department. But there was another guy already talking to her—balding, Cubs baseball cap, a few years older than me—and the two of them seemed friendly.

Not that I had any intention of admitting this to anyone, ever, but I also kind of lost my nerve. She was so *different* here than she'd been outside the bar or in her classroom. So open, friendly, relaxed...vulnerable. I guess I just couldn't take seeing her stiffen up the way she would the second she saw me.

Plus, it was fun spying on her and seeing her so unguarded. She was one of those naturally beautiful women who didn't seem to realize they were beautiful. Her dark hair fell in soft waves. Her eyes sparkled with warmth as she talked to the other guy. Her smile was kind and genuine.

Damn. I was kind of jealous of that.

I just couldn't bring myself to mess up the moment for her.

So I actually snuck away. Grabbed my box of rotini pasta, a jar of sauce, and a container of parmesan cheese, and then I checked out in the express lane before she noticed me.

I hadn't done something like that—run away from a girl—since I was, like... Hell. I couldn't even remember. Twelve, maybe? Why did I suddenly feel like a junior-high kid around her?

Then I got home and made the mistake of reading my texts. And listening to my messages.

"Where the heck are you?" my sister demanded in her voicemail message, after having sent about seven texts. "You skipped a family gathering! Are you dead?" she sniped. "In the hospital? Being held at gunpoint? If not, call me."

Oh, shit.

So, I called her. "Sorry, Shar. I forgot about this one. But I just saw you all on Monday."

"*That* was for your birthday," she retorted. "*This* is because it's 9-11. We need to remember the heroes and those we lost by honoring our family, the people we love, and our country."

I was as patriotic as the next guy but, seriously, I didn't see how a Friday fish fry was going to help us remember the fallen.

"Well, I can honor you tomorrow instead," I told her.

"Tonight I'm staying at home, watching TV, and crashing early."

"Tomorrow, I'm going to Drew's with my friends, so you're on your own," she said with a huff. "Don't miss the next family dinner, Blake." She paused. "I love you, you know."

"I know. I love you, too, Sis."

Of course, the next night, when I was driving down Main Street, I glanced over at Drew's Diner. I knew Shar would be in there, but as I looked through the large bay window, just who was standing next to her? That's right. The French teacher. Two nights in a row.

So, given how the week was going, it shouldn't have surprised me at all that I'd run into Vicky on Sunday morning while I was taking Winston for a walk in Eastman Field.

Seriously, this chick was *everywhere*.

My chest tightened and my throat went dry the second I spotted her. She was a vision in black spandex. Headphones on. Striding down the walking path with purpose. Evasion was possible, but I'd had enough of backing away.

"*Bonjour,* Mademoiselle," I said, intercepting her. Winston barked merrily at her sneaker-clad feet.

Her eyes widened as she took in the sight of me and my dog. Pulling out her earbuds, she stared at me for a long moment before clearing her throat. "Uh, Blake. Hi." She then turned her gaze to Winston and, at last, smiled. "Hey, who's this?"

"This would be Winston. He's more exuberant than polite," I said as my canine ball of fluff tugged at his leash, trying to get closer to her. "But he's generally well intentioned." I held him back—he clearly wanted to lavish her with wet kisses, and I couldn't blame him—but Vicky knelt down in front of him and held out her hand. Winston immediately nuzzled it with his nose and then licked every one of her fingers.

She petted his tangled curls and laughed. It was a lovely sound.

"What a cutie you are," she whispered to him in a soft, sweet tone I hadn't heard her use before. For a second, I was envious of my dog.

Winston reveled in the attention. He wagged his tail like a frenzied rudder, so hard and fast that I thought it might start propelling him around the park. He rolled on his back to let her rub his belly. A true show of trust, especially in one so hyper.

"Wow," I said. "He likes you."

"How long have you had him?" Vicky asked.

"Not quite a month. He's a rescue. The vet thinks he's about a year old."

She finally stood up and gazed at me with big, surprised eyes. "Really? You rescued him?"

I didn't know why that should shock her so much, so I just nodded.

"He's beautiful. What made you decide to get him?"

"I—uh..."

It was rare that I was at a loss for words, but it was hard to explain why I'd even walked into the animal shelter that day. It was a spur of the moment thing. But I stepped inside and glanced around, and the second my eyes and Winston's met, I just *knew* we belonged to each other. Verbalizing that would sound weird, though.

After a moment, I managed to say, "I just really like dogs."

She squinted at me. It was clear that she approved of my mutt, but the skeptical expression on her face clued me that she still wasn't much of a fan of *me*.

I decided to turn the conversation over to her. "So, what are you listening to? Jazz? Classical? Heavy metal? Rap?" I pointed to her earbuds. I couldn't see the device they were attached to. It had to be hidden somewhere in her clothing.

Not that I could tell where. Everything she was wearing was sleek and formfitting—the way workout clothes should be, in my opinion. Especially the way her shirt clung to her fine breasts and her leggings hugged her ass. *I* wanted to hug her ass like that. Mmm.

"None of the above," she retorted, her voice several degrees cooler than before. Man, she was touchy.

"World music then? Some French singer?"

"Would you know their names if I listed a few?" She cocked one eyebrow at me in challenge.

Thing was, I worked as a DJ. I'd actually listened to quite a lot of musical artists, including several French singers—soloists, rock bands, even folksy stuff. But it would make it too easy on her if I told her that. Besides, she seemed to enjoy labeling me as a cultural idiot. Why spoil her fun so soon?

"Why don't you enlighten me, Mademoiselle?" There was, maybe, a little bite to my response, but if she heard it, she didn't acknowledge it.

She shook her head. "I wasn't listening to music at all," she said smugly. "Many times when I walk, I listen to audiobooks instead."

She shrugged in a way that indicated that she didn't think I'd understand the concept. That I was the kind of guy who must not like reading.

This pissed me off. Big time. She didn't know who she was dealing with here.

I exhaled, crossed my arms, and pulled myself to my full height, just so I could look down at her a little more. "Excellent," I said with exaggerated confidence. "I've been looking for someone to talk to about the latest fiction *New York Times* bestsellers. I've only read, maybe, six out of this week's top ten so far, but I just downloaded *The Gatekeeper* by Benson Sallari. It's been number one in mainstream thrillers for the past three weeks. Have you read—or listened—to it?"

She narrowed her eyes at me. "Not yet."

"More into lit fic, then? I really liked *Seventh House* by Eliza Castillo. They're making a movie out of that one." I stared at her in question.

She shook her head.

"No on that book, too? How about Brett Butzman's *A Ride Through Provence*? Katriona Gayle's *Counting Sheep*? Or A.J. Weston's latest mystery, *The Clock Strikes Back*? Surely, you've read at least one of those, right?" I did my best to sound superior.

"I've h-heard of them, of course," she stuttered. "But I've been listening to something historical lately."

"Oh, that Henry the 8th biography by Nelson Oakes? Everyone's been talking about that. I finished it in, like, two days. Impressive research, don't you think?"

"I wouldn't know. The book I've been listening to isn't a major bestseller, but it's entertaining."

"An entertaining historical that isn't a bestseller? You've stumped me."

"It's a Regency love story."

"Wait. A romance novel? Really?" I snorted. "For someone as highbrow and sophisticated as *you*, Mademoiselle? I'm shocked."

I wasn't remotely shocked. Of course she'd be a romance lover. Despite her cultural interests and her intelligence, Vicky Bernier probably wanted what most single women wanted: A white knight to rescue them and fall in love with them and recite dreadful poetry to them or sing Barry Connelly's crappy love songs to them. Much as I had a soft spot in my heart for genre fiction—mysteries, sci-fi/fantasies, thrillers, and more—general romance novels were no better than the songs I had to play on 102.5 every day, only a helluva lot longer.

"I enjoy a range of reading material, Blake," she said stiffly. "I don't consider romance to be remotely lowbrow. Some of the greatest minds in English literature wrote romantic novels. Jane Austen, for instance. Or the Brontë sisters—"

I snorted again. "Mr. Rochester and that Heathcliff dude were about as romantic as my ass. I'm telling you, those Brontë bitches were messed up if they thought any woman would fall in love with some drunk, foul-tempered douchebag."

"Well, I guess you'd know," she shot back.

Ouch.

I had to give her credit for a fast comeback but, wow, she didn't pull punches.

"I suppose I set myself up for that," I murmured.

She shrugged, slipped her earbuds back in, and said only, "Bye," as she bolted down the walking path.

Winston barked after her, and I felt a sudden sharp pang of disappointment at her absence. And, I had to admit, an even sharper stab of regret at having been the one to drive her away.

I knew Vicky hadn't thought highly of me before, but I could see now that it was more personal than I'd suspected. It wasn't just that she was uptight. Maybe Shar had prejudiced her against me. Maybe she'd had a few negative opinions based on hearing me on the air. I didn't know. But I was sure now that she'd judged me harshly after seeing the bar fight last week. And that her first impressions weren't likely to easily change.

The competitor in me wanted to try, though. Just because it was in my nature not to back down from a battle. Just because I wanted to see if I could. And just because— aw, hell—the truth was that I was starting to like her, and I wished she would like me back. Even a little.

My sister had a gift for being a loving but painful thorn

in my side.

"Seriously, Shar?" I said when she called my cell *the very second* the Bears kicked off against the Packers that afternoon. I'd just gotten comfy on the sofa: Beer on my left, potato chips on my right, the remote control on my lap, and the game on the big screen in front of me. "Do you not realize what's on right now?"

"Oh, I realize it, all right. That's why I'm calling. I knew you'd be home," my little sister said smugly.

"What do you want to nag me about this time?" I said, cringing when I saw the Bears quarterback go down in a massive pile on before he'd even managed to make the first play. This didn't bode well.

"I'm not nagging," Shar said defensively in my ear, effectively making me miss the sports commentary on that disastrous first down. "I just want you to try to be on your best behavior with my friends. Please. Especially Vicky."

"Well, she wasn't on her best behavior with me," I said, watching a painful replay of the second-down pass that resulted in an unsuccessful attempt to gain yardage. "Damn."

"Damn, what?" Shar chirped.

"It's just—what were we talking about?"

"Being nice to Vicky."

"Oh, that. Look, Sis, she's not a bad person or anything." I thought about the French teacher for a second. She was smart, gorgeous, kind to my dog. These weren't observations I intended to share with my sister, though. "But she's high strung, a total rule follower, uptight, snappish—"

"Snappish? *Vicky?* Are we talking about the *same* woman?"

I remembered her comment this morning about me being like a dickhead Brontë "hero," and I shuddered a little at the memory. Did she really see me like that? Not that I'd confide shit in my meddlesome little sister, but her friend's comments kind of niggled, even though I could see why Vicky had gotten that impression of me. The thing that bothered me most, though, was the way the French teacher had assumed I was unread and uncultured. I wouldn't debate being seen as a douche or a drinker, but being seen as dumb really pissed me off.

"How well do you actually know her, Shar? I mean, are you aware that she's prickly, judgmental, has a ton of angry feelings and unresolved issues with men—"

"She's *sensitive*, Blake. And what single woman in her thirties doesn't have issues with men?" She huffed on the line. "I know you're a good guy deep down. *Very* deep down. You keep it well hidden, but I know that goodness is in there. Our brothers know it, too, and so does your dog. Other people have no clue, though, and when you go out of your way to aggravate someone—"

"Okay, fine. So, maybe I did go out of my way to piss off Vicky, but she started it."

Crap. I sounded like a four-year-old kid. This fact wasn't lost on my sister.

"Jesus, Blake. Grow up. How will anybody ever see your good qualities if you don't start acting like an adult? And I don't mean that fakey radio-jock façade you put on in public to show off either."

"Fakey? I'm not—"

"You are. And talk about anger issues. You're the king of them. No wonder you recognized that in Vicky."

I glanced at the TV and took a long swig of beer, trying to calm down, ground myself, and figure out what to say next. Somehow, the Packers had managed to score in the first five minutes of the first quarter. Shit.

I clicked off the game and downed the rest of my beer. Then I reached for another one. Yes, I was angry, and not just because the Bears were getting the crap beaten out of them today. My sister's accusations stung. If anyone knew what I'd suffered by losing both parents, she did.

But Shar and I had reacted in different ways. She coped by surrounding herself with people all the freakin' time. She knew what she wanted out of life and loved the profession she'd chosen. She'd felt a deep loss when Mom and Dad died only a few years apart, of course, but she wasn't the type to dwell in sadness for long. She always seemed so sure that she could affect change, "make a difference," bring everyone together, create a new reality just by her sheer will.

And, bless her, she usually could.

But she couldn't shape and manage and corral me into doing what she wanted all the time. No matter how much she thought it was in my best interests. And I knew that ticked her off.

Telling her this was, however, futile, so I just let her blather on about how I needed to take better care of myself, try to avoid meaningless relationships, and stop abusing my body with booze and junk food.

I grabbed a few potato chips and crunched them loud enough by the phone to make sure she could hear me.

"Blake!"

"Oh, c'mon, Shar. Just chill. You're starting to sound as scolding and schoolmarmish as your little Frenchie friend."

And then, just because I *was* angry and had enough of being told what to do, I said something I knew would wound her. "Maybe Chandler had the right idea. Just blow the hell out of Mirabelle Harbor and stay away for *years* at a time. No one giving him orders. No one interfering in his life."

"Please don't say that," she whispered.

"Fine. I won't say it. But lay off me. I mean it, Shar. You know it was never my plan to still be here."

I let that hang in the air between us. Let her ponder that reality, which she'd never wanted to acknowledge, even though it was the truth. But I knew she remembered. That insinuation Vicky lobbed at me about not being well read or well traveled or remotely cultured or worldly or adventurous, etc., that stung, too. Because, even though I'd only taken French for a couple of years and Spanish for a couple more, I had a knack for languages. I would have traveled all over the world if I could have. It'd been a dream of mine.

I'd had a two-month European and Asian backpacking trip planned seven years ago, just before Dad got diagnosed with his cancer. None of us wanted to leave our parents alone during that ordeal, so I postponed the trip and stayed home. Worked at a gas station all summer instead, just so I could be nearby. Figured I'd go on the trip a year or two later.

But just when I began setting up travel arrangements again, Mom died of a sudden stroke. Chandler, having had enough family tragedy, only lasted in town for a few weeks before leaving like Meatloaf's "Bat Out of Hell." He took off with Abby, his girlfriend at the time, but he was so restless that even she couldn't handle drifting through five years and half a dozen states... She cut him loose somewhere in Florida. She stayed there, and he still hadn't come back home either.

Shar was bereft after Mom died. Her marriage was falling apart then, and I couldn't leave her, too. So I canceled the second trip. Figured it was a sign or something. Every time I tried to get out of Mirabelle Harbor someone died or something really bad happened. Didn't want to risk it again.

I heard Shar sigh on the line. "I'm sorry, Blake. I feel like a broken record, and I know I'm being pushy. But I truly care about you, and I want you to be safe. Healthy. Happy. That's all, okay?"

My temper was starting to fizzle with the sadness and resignation in her voice. Shar was a tough cookie, but she was easy to bruise if you knew how. And I knew how.

"Hey, sorry to worry you so much, Sis. Just...don't

mind me today. I'm not in a great mood. Or in a great place in my life."

"How can I help?"

"You can tell your friend to lighten up," I joked.

"Do you really not like her or want to work with her, Blake? Because it's not worth doing the Homecoming dance if it's going to be such a stressor on you both. Maybe ask if another DJ can do it that night, okay? I had no idea you wouldn't like Vicky this much."

"It's not that...exactly. I don't *dislike* her, Shar. But I know she doesn't like me. And you're right," I conceded. "I haven't given her much reason to."

"Well, if anyone can charm someone, you can." She laughed suddenly, seemingly delighted to point out such an obvious solution, in her opinion. "Just show her how cool and clever you are. She's a nice person. She'll respond to that."

For the first time since she called, I actually grinned and put down my beer. My sister might be overly optimistic about my ability to win over her straight-laced friend, but I knew there was something I could do that just might help out Vicky's students and, possibly, make her see me in a more favorable light.

Then again, I could just as easily crash and burn as badly as the Bears today.

"I'll think about it," I told Shar. "I have a couple of ideas. But I make no promises."

CHAPTER SEVEN

~*Vicky*~

I'd just returned to my classroom Tuesday early afternoon, following a foreign language department meeting over lunch with Lisa, Christine, Marcie, and Janet.

We'd ordered pizza and hashed out the majority of activities for November's "International Week," when foreign exchange students from around the state came to visit Mirabelle Harbor High School for a few days. The event took some planning, but it was always exciting for the kids and it tended to be one of the highlights of the year.

So, I was still smiling when the intercom buzzed and our school secretary said, "Ms. Bernier, you've got a phone call on line one. Do you have time to take it?"

"Sure." I had about ten minutes before the next class started arriving. She transferred the call and I said, "Hello?"

"Mademoiselle Bernier," a distinctive voice said. The guy had a way of even making my name sound sinful.

"Mr. Michaelsen," I replied with a sigh. "What a

surprise to hear from you. Again. So soon."

He chuckled—a sound so deep and sensual that I could feel the vibrations to the tips of my toenails. What was it about his voice that just got to me? Without the distraction of seeing him face to face, I couldn't help but concentrate on the sound. If ever a man had been born to be on the radio, Blake was it.

He cleared his throat. "The reason I'm calling you at school is because I have a free promotional opportunity for your Homecoming committee. But, before I took things any further, I wanted to run the idea by you. I figured you weren't the type to want anything sprung on you at the last minute."

That wasn't an accusation, precisely, but—coming from Blake—it wasn't quite a compliment either. He may as well have just said, *Since you're so boring and not very spontaneous...*

"I—um, thanks," I said. "I appreciate your thoughtfulness." Which, I did, I guess. "What does it entail?"

"A buddy of mine is a freelance sports writer. He often has pieces in the *Chicago Tribune* or the *Sun-Times*, and he writes a short weekly sports column for the *Mirabelle Harbor Gazette*. His name is Declan Night. You've probably heard of him, yes?"

The name sounded sort of familiar, but I hadn't made a habit of paying much attention to athletic types. "Is he a baseball player?" I guessed.

Blake laughed.

"Uh, football...maybe?"

"Try hockey," he said. "Pro hockey. Dec grew up around here and then moved to Colorado to play for a while. Then he was traded and spent a few years out East until he did some shit to his shoulder and had to call it quits. But he's living in town now and doing a bunch of things—some game commentary, some writing, some sports retail."

"Does he want to sell t-shirts or something during Homecoming Week?" I asked.

Blake laughed again, harder this time. "No. But, as a favor to Coach Fortin, who's a second cousin of his or something, Dec was planning on coming to the high school this week to write up a feature on the football team as they prep for the new season and the big Homecoming game. He's going to have a photographer with him, and we could easily ask another reporter from the *Gazette,* who's a mutual friend of ours, to tag along and make an afternoon of it. Write up a short piece about the Homecoming planning committee and their fundraising efforts. Do you think you and the kids would like that?"

"Wow. Yeah. They'd love it, and I would, too, of course," I said honestly, wondering why it had never occurred to me to reach out to the local press. As the advisor, I should have thought of that.

Then again, Blake was a true Michaelsen. I'd underestimated him, of course—not only his intelligence but, also, his degree of connectedness.

I shouldn't have.

Shar was one of the strongest networkers I'd ever met, and I should have guessed that her brother would be the same, if not more so.

"Great," he said. "I'll tell Declan and the guys that it's a go for Thursday after school. As I recall, the committee is meeting again then. I'll also bring the song list I promised the students."

"Thank you, Blake. I don't know what to say. That's just—"

"Incredibly impressive and thoughtful of me?" he suggested in a cocky tone. He didn't wait for me to reply. "Yeah, I know. For the record, I'm not the evil troll you've taken me for, Babe."

"For the record," I mimicked, "do not call me 'Babe.'

Ever."

He laughed a laugh that was totally unrepentant. "Or what? You'll make me sit in the corner? Oooh, no wait— this is better. You'll tie me to your desk and we'll play the 'Naughty School Boy/Strict Teacher' game. Have you got a ruler, some rope and, maybe, a little masking tape?"

The image that flooded my mind made every part of me blush. I was so glad he couldn't see me, although I suspected he could tell just how flustered I must be. It was impossible for me to separate my embarrassment from my desire. He seemed determined to bring out both in me, simultaneously. I couldn't help but feel an unwanted but undeniable attraction to the far-too-charming DJ.

But I knew I couldn't let him get away with saying these things. Couldn't let him think that just because he came up with one thoughtful and responsible idea that it excused his every other immature or inappropriate action.

I took a deep breath. "We're on a school phone line, Blake. Please keep your BDSM fantasies to yourself."

He burst out laughing again. Then, in a low, sexy voice, he whispered, "Then give me your cell number instead, so I can call you privately."

The guy was incorrigible.

I hung up before I could incriminate myself or before he could actually talk me into giving him my number. I got the sense that Blake Michaelsen was used to getting his way with women. A lot.

Philippe had been a charmer like that, too. So had a handful of the ex-boyfriends that followed. In fact, looking back, almost every man I'd ever fallen for had been more flash and enchanting illusion than substance.

After my painful breakup with Philippe, who'd been "Mr. Culture" (at least on the outside), I'd swung too far to the other extreme. Especially when I dated Ryan, a tax attorney, whose love of numbers was eclipsed only by his love of college football and cheap beer. It was a wonder our relationship even lasted two full months.

That had been a low point in my dating life, and it succeeded in making me certain that I'd stay forever single. I didn't seem to be the right fit for anybody. I'd been hurt by Philippe, bored by Ryan, and utterly indifferent to most other guys. So, since I refused to have one-night stands, that meant it'd been over eighteen months since I'd had a sexual experience that wasn't battery operated.

This, I knew, was what had to be fueling any attraction I might feel toward Blake. It *had* to be. No one on the planet was less right for me than that guy. Although, I guess I had to give him credit for reading a lot. And for rescuing a dog. He got points for both of these. But, as we all knew, even a broken grandfather clock could tell the right time twice a day.

Blake was stunningly like a six-foot-two broken clock.

With a gorgeous exterior.

And a dreamy voice.

But, *mon Dieu!*

Even if he was the hottest man in the room (which I suspected he often was), and even if he'd read every book on the *New York Times* Bestseller List (which seemed to be his goal), and even if he hadn't made fun of romance (which he did), or made a habit out of stirring up trouble (which was a gift of his, whether it was in my classroom or in downtown Mirabelle Harbor), he *still* wouldn't be my type.

Because he was crude.

And reckless.

And egocentric.

Too much of a little boy in grownup clothing.

And all that reading didn't make him interested in the wider world and its people. I'd bet he was one of those guys who took only enough Spanish in school to order fajita toppings.

I couldn't imagine him speaking a word of French—at

least not one that wasn't either an insult or a come on.

But even if he turned out to be fluent in eight languages, wrote to pen pals on six continents, and was a charter member of several international peace-keeping organizations, I knew better than to get suckered into a relationship with a charmer like Blake. Period.

"Bonjour, Mademoiselle," Blake said to me on Thursday afternoon as he waltzed into my classroom a few minutes ahead of my Homecoming committee members.

He was flanked by three men—they made a quartet of tall, athletic-looking thirty-somethings. The four of them together looked like they were ripped from the pages of *GQ*'s Sports and Casualwear Collection and tossed unsuspectingly into the middle of Mirabelle Harbor High School.

"Nous sommes ici," Blake continued in surprisingly strong French, as if he'd read my mind on Tuesday and couldn't wait to show me up. *"Pour une introduction officielle—"* He pointed to the hockey player, whose face I realized I recognized from the media, and said, *"Il s'appelle* Declan Night." Then, turning toward the other two men, he added, *"Ceci est un photographe excellent,* Geoff Everest, *et un autre journaliste,* Trevor Cayne." He grinned at me. *"Ah, mes amis, c'est mon plaisir de revenir à l'école secondaire de vous présenter à* Mademoiselle Vicky Bernier. *Elle est très—"*

"Knock it off with the French, Blake," I said, probably more sharply than necessary, but he was clearly showing off. And I had no idea what he was going to tell his friends about me. Any sentence that began with *"Elle est très..." She is very...* was a dangerous opening.

"What? Does my pronunciation suck?" he said. "I

mean, I may be a little rusty, but I thought—"

"It was fine," I told him, which was a blatant lie. His pronunciation was better than most of my fourth-year Advanced Placement students, but he didn't need a bigger head than the one he had already. "However, the students will be here any minute," I added, which was true. "So we should get set up." I avoided Blake's gaze and smiled at each of the other men. "It's very nice to meet you, Declan, Geoff, and Trevor. Please call me Vicky."

Blake shot me a scowl but he then began directing his posse of American heartthrobs around the room.

"Geoff, why don't you set up your tripod in that open space at the back?" he suggested. "And Trev, there will only be about four kids coming, so we can pull a few desks together—whatever formation works best for you for the interview." He turned to the former hockey star. "What do you want to do, Dec? Hang out here for a while or head out to the football field?"

Declan jabbed his thumb toward the hall. "I've actually gotta talk to the coaches for a few minutes while the players dress and warm up. So, I'll be in the locker rooms until practice starts. Trev, I'll see you back at the paper. Thanks for coming out."

The other journalist nodded as he pulled out his laptop from his bag. "No prob, Dec."

"And, Geoff, when you're finished up here, just meet me on the field," Declan added.

"We can start with the photos," Blake suggested, "so he can get down to the team sooner."

"Great." Declan smiled at me. "Nice to meet you, Vicky."

"Likewise," I said.

To his buddies from the *Gazette*, Declan waved, and to Blake he fake pounded on his shoulder with a clenched fist. "See ya later, man."

Blake faux punched him back. "Stay awesome, dude."

"You know it." The hockey guy laughed as he left the room.

Not ten seconds later, Matt burst through the door. "I just saw Declan Night! In our hallway!" The junior class president caught Blake's eye and grinned. "Do you know him?"

"Yep. He's a good guy." Blake nodded at Stephanie, Alexis, and Heath as they joined us in the classroom. Then, to all the kids, he said, "I brought some friends here today." He introduced the reporter and the camera guy and explained about the *Mirabelle Harbor Gazette*'s Homecoming feature.

"Oh, cool!" Alexis glanced between the men and then over at Heath. "So, we're all gonna be in the paper, too?"

Blake nodded and helped the students get set up for a short photo shoot with Geoff.

"Yo, Heath. You wanna comb down that hair?" Matt joked. The other guy's straight dark hair was spiked in every direction, like porcupine quills.

Heath laughed and directed a rather rude gesture at the class president. The artistic boy didn't chitchat a lot, but he could express himself just fine.

Alexis reached out to gently tug at a spiked strand. "I like it this way." She and Heath shared a smile, and the boy blushed.

Ah. So they'd definitely gotten closer over the past week. I wasn't surprised. Teen relationships moved at the speed of a Twitter thread. And I was happy for them. I just hoped their courtship lasted long enough to make it all the way through Homecoming Week. I didn't want the committee to implode with adolescent drama before the dance came to a close.

Blake surveyed the students. "You all look fantastic."

Geoff snapped a couple of tester shots, just to focus the kids' attention on the camera.

Blake said, "Hey, don't forget the advisor."

It took me a second to realize he was talking about me. "Oh, no, no. That's fine. I'm just—"

"The head of the Homecoming committee," Blake interjected. "You need to be in the picture."

"And you should be in here, too, Blake," Stephanie piped up. "You're part of our team now as well."

She looked at him so sweetly, so earnestly, that I saw Blake pause. He swallowed and his usual smirky expression softened. "I, uh, well, if it's all right with your teacher."

All the students looked at me expectantly.

"Of course," I said.

Blake sent me a grateful look. Did he actually think I'd be so mean as to exclude him from something like this? Maybe I'd been too harsh on him in the past week. He must think I was disapproving of *everything* he did. I wasn't. But he was just so...so cocky and flippant, and I didn't know what to do with someone like that.

Geoff had us stand like bookends with the four kids between us. He snapped a handful of shots like that, got us to change poses and, suddenly, I found myself right next to Blake, with his arm around my shoulders.

I froze as his hand lightly caressed my upper arm. The second Geoff stopped taking pictures, I jumped away from Blake. He raised one amused eyebrow at me and the corners of his lips tilted upward.

See? This was exactly the kind of thing that drove me nuts. You'd give a guy like Blake an inch, and he'd take a mile and a half.

Thankfully, the kids didn't seem to notice the irritation I was feeling. The photographer packed up and left and Trevor took over, asking the students about the planned Homecoming Week activities, taking copious notes on his laptop, and double checking every detail—time, place, event—to make sure he recorded it correctly. He was good with the students. Not quite as jovial and chatty as Blake tended to be, but Trevor was very straight with them, taking them seriously, like the adults they were on the verge of becoming. I knew the kids appreciated that.

When Trevor asked about the theme of the dance, Alexis explained that it was "The Eighties."

A funny grin crossed the reporter's face. He turned to me. "You trust this guy to play only *good* tunes?" He poked his index finger at Blake.

"Trev," Blake said with a warning tone.

"Hey, you forget, I remember you at my sister's wedding." Trevor crossed his arms and addressed the rest of us. "He was the DJ at the reception, and I'm pretty sure *no one* in the wedding party had requested Snoop Dogg and Pharrell's 'Drop It Like It's Hot' during the dance."

Blake chuckled. "Oh, c'mon. It's not like the garter toss is a *dignified* part of the wedding tradition."

Trevor started laughing, so much so that his shoulders shook from it and his eyes got a bit watery. "I never told you this, Blake, but my sister's new mother-in-law spent, like, the next hour trying to puzzle out the lyrics." He swiped at the corners of his eyes. "You try to explain to someone who's never listened to rap that 'ice cubes' and 'ice creams' aren't things you'd find in the freezer."

All of us burst out laughing at that. I knew only a handful of rap songs, but I'd watched my share of music videos, especially when I was in college. Enough to know that "ice cubes" were diamonds and "ice creams" were a brand of shoes. And that the song in question was a supremely bawdy tune.

"You'd better let me read your playlist in advance, Blake," I said, doing my best to sound serious.

"Got it right here." He pulled out a folded sheet of paper from his back pocket and shot me a look of pride.

I scanned the song titles—mostly big Eighties hits. "Say You, Say Me" by Lionel Richie. "Magic" by The Cars. "You're the Inspiration" by Chicago. And the like.

"What's this one? 'Love Bites' by Def Leppard?" I asked.

"Yeah, what about it?" Blake said. "It's from the Eighties. And it's a love ballad. Kind of."

I rolled my eyes. "Not exactly. But these all look fine. Just don't deviate from this list."

"What if I get a special request?"

"Then run it by me first. I'll be there. The *whole* time. Listening attentively." I hoped I sounded suitably threatening.

He winked at me and flashed three of his fingers upward, like a Boy Scout in a show of oath-taking. "I promise I won't deviate. Scout's honor."

"You were never a Boy Scout, Blake," Trevor said with a grin. "I've known you for fourteen years, and I distinctly remember you saying at a bar once that joining the Scouts was like—"

Blake jumped up and clapped his palm over his buddy's mouth. "I think that's enough reminiscing, Trev. What do you say we get back to the interview, eh?"

The reporter pushed Blake's hand away and chuckled. "Yeah, sure. But you'll owe me a beer later for my silence." He glanced at me. "Because I think I have a few stories that Vicky here would be *very interested* in hearing, and I'm sure the teens would—"

"I owe you two beers and a platter of loaded nachos," Blake interrupted. "Now, stop blackmailing me and finish the damn interview."

Trevor refreshed his screen and typed a few words into the document. "Okay, where were we? The dance theme, right?"

By the time the reporter was ready to leave, he'd shaped the collection of details thrown at him by the kids into a solid outline for his newspaper piece.

"This'll run next Friday or Saturday," he told us. "I'll make sure it gets in the *Gazette* before Homecoming Week starts." He swiveled toward Blake as the students started to file out of the room. "D'ya wanna put in any direct plugs for the radio station? Give Doug and Leonard something happy to read with their morning espressos?"

Blake nodded. "You're a pain in the ass, Trev, but a genius. And, yeah, the bosses would like that. Just say the usual—102.5 is honored to be the official musical sponsor of Homecoming, etc., etc., and maybe add in some pithy slogan like...I don't know." He paused and rubbed his temples. "Something besides that lame old 'Nothing but love, 24/7.' They've way overused that." He paused again. "How about 102.5 LOVE FM, The Heartbeat of Mirabelle Harbor?"

"Oh, that's good," Trevor said, fast typing. "Consider it done." He closed his computer, gathered his things, and man-hugged Blake. "This weekend. Beer at Max's. Text me."

"You got it. Thanks, man," Blake said.

The reporter and I shook hands, and I thanked him for taking the time to come in.

"Hey, any friend of this jackass is a friend of mine. Hope you have fun at the dance. But if you need any other Blake Michaelsen stories, I've got—"

"Out!" Blake commanded. "Or you'll be owing *me* beers this weekend."

Trevor left, and I could still hear him laughing halfway down the hall.

And then there were two.

Blake regarded me with an almost serious expression. "So, was this good?"

I nodded. "Thanks for arranging it for all of us. I could tell the kids were really thrilled."

He shrugged off the praise. "Nothing much to it, Vicky. Glad you feel this helped them out a little." He hadn't brought a lot with him. A leather jacket. His phone. Some keys. He started to collect them. He'd be leaving soon, too.

For some strange reason, I didn't want him to go just yet.

"And, um, thanks for that song list," I added, trying to extend the conversation.

He paused and half smiled at me. "Natch."

I waved the sheet of paper at him. "So...do you have a favorite song on here? I mean, what musicians from that era did you like? Madonna, Michael Jackson, Culture Club?"

He cringed. "That would be 'D'—None of the above." But he put his keys back down on the student desk and leaned against it as I scanned the song list.

"Van Halen?" I tried. "Duran Duran?"

"No, and hell no."

"What about Huey Lewis and the News?"

"Eh, they weren't too bad," he admitted. "A few of their tunes were kind of catchy, actually."

"Like 'Do You Believe in Love?'" I said.

"Not *that* one."

I laughed. "Why not, Blake? Too poppish? Too upbeat?"

"Too much of a lie," he shot back, a look I couldn't gauge crossing his handsome face and darkening his expression.

Whoa.

Where had this mood come from? And why was it showing up now...once everyone else had left? There was a simmering anger about something, just beneath the surface of Blake's confident and ultra-social veneer. I thought back on what he'd just said and tried to puzzle out what, exactly, had set him off.

"You're saying you don't believe in love?"

"I'm not a romance fan like you, Mademoiselle," he replied in a low voice. "I'd rather just call the feeling what it is: A combination of lust, desire, possessiveness, obsession, fantasy, overdependence, self-delusion, weakness..." His lips twisted into something that vaguely resembled a smile, but I wasn't fooled. It was much more like a grimace. "Not that the experience doesn't have its charms," he added. "At least in the short term."

I thought about my parents and their life-long true love story. I thought about some of my friends, too, who'd had decades of love and commitment with their significant others. And I thought about the fictional heroes and heroines, which were dreamed up by real people, who had to draw their relationship inspiration from somewhere, right? Love wasn't *always* a fantasy. I didn't think every love story could be reduced to a case of "lust" meeting "overdependence," either.

I put down the song list. "That makes me sad," I told him. "That you look at all relationships that way."

"Hey, don't knock it 'til you try it," he said lightly. "A one-night—or, hey, even a two- or three-night stand has a lot to recommend it." He motioned me closer, like he was going to tell me a secret.

I took a step near him and leaned in.

"Wanna grab a drink with me, Vicky? *Voulez-vous prendre un verre avec moi?*" He paused. "Then...go back to my place and get naked? Hmm? Could be fun." He raised a dark eyebrow to go along with this unlikely invitation.

I stepped back immediately and shook my head. He was probably just toying with me anyway. Propositioning me just to see what I'd say or do.

"Do women ever agree to that, Blake?" Although I knew that, of course, they did. Especially with someone like him.

He shrugged. "You'd be surprised, Mademoiselle."

"Well, I'm sure you *won't* be surprised that I'm not someone who would. Sorry to turn down your offer."

"For now," he murmured.

A laugh caught in my throat. I had to give the guy credit for persistence. "I'm not likely to change my mind, you know."

"Maybe, maybe not," he said, a small grin returning to his lips. He grabbed his things and strode to the door. "But 'not likely' isn't an absolute no. There's some wiggle room there." With a wink and an *à bientôt*—a "see you soon" that came across as equal parts perilous threat and tantalizing promise—he was gone.

CHAPTER EIGHT

~*Blake*~

I spent the weekend engaging in my new favorite pastime: Running into Vicky Bernier around town.

I knew her habits now and where to find her. Spotted her on Friday evening at Mirabelle Market. Waved at her this time. Her first instinct was to scowl at me, but her good manners took over and she reluctantly waved back.

Went to Max's Pub with Trevor on Saturday night. Saw Vicky with a pair of girlfriends walking into The Lounge next door. Teachers and their imported wine. Was tempted to get plastered, but just thinking about her in the next establishment over, judging me, was kind of a buzz kill.

Spotted a few women at the bar that I might have tried to pick up in the past. Trev was sure hitting on them hard, and I knew he'd likely end up going home with a hot redhead. But I couldn't get Vicky out of my mind. She probably had no idea I was nearby, but I didn't want to even chance her spotting me leaving Max's Pub with some other chick. Or have her see me walking out into the square falling-down drunk, like last time.

The whole damn thing was irritating as hell, actually. Here I was, staying on my best behavior for a woman who didn't even know I wanted to please her. A woman I wasn't even dating. Fucking insane.

Trev, who liked to have an occasional smoke when we'd go out, said, "I need a cigarette. Wanna stand outside with me for five minutes?"

"Why don't you ask your lady friend to keep you company?" I glanced around. "Where'd Ms. Red go anyway?"

He inclined his head just slightly in the direction of a corner table. The redhead was chatting it up with another guy. "I think she's playing hard to get. I wanna see if she notices that I'm not where she last saw me. If she looks around for me."

So I shrugged and followed my buddy out into the mid-September night.

As he lit up, I gazed through the windows of the bar next door and saw Vicky at a table with her friends. She glanced outside right at that moment, and I was irrationally glad that Trevor had dragged me out here.

I was tempted to smile at her, but I didn't. She looked away, pretending she hadn't seen me. But I knew she had. The owners of the wine bar kept those windows good and clean.

"She noticed," Trev said.

"Yeah, I know," I replied. But, though he was talking about Ms. Red, who was looking frantically around Max's for him, I was thinking about Vicky.

Only difference was that Trev would get laid tonight, and I wouldn't.

Which was one of the reasons why I was in an edgier mood than usual the next morning. Sunday. 11:30ish. Time to take Winston on a walk to the park.

And Vicky was a beautiful creature of habit. I'd seen her exercise walking here last week at this time...and, oh, yeah. There she was now. Like clockwork. Striding around the sidewalks by Eastman Field. In her skintight Lycra workout clothes.

I *loved* Lycra.

She was on the straightaway closest to the lake, heading north and focused entirely on her audiobook.

I grinned. I'd had enough of being ignored by her. And Winston, upon spotting her, gave a friendly bark.

He wasn't accustomed to being ignored either. I let him off of his leash and said, "You wanna go say hi to the pretty lady?" I pointed toward Vicky then gave Winston a reassuring pat. "You go say hello!"

My dog barked again and took off, bounding with enthusiasm toward his target. I laughed and jogged after him. Then watched as Winston intercepted Vicky, wagging his tail hard and licking her hand the second she stopped, bent down, and reached out to pet him.

Her gaze connected with mine and, this time, she didn't pretend not to see me. Ah, progress.

"Hey, there, Mademoiselle. Have fun at The Lounge last night?"

She looked momentarily flustered by the question but disguised it by burying her head in Winston's fur. My dog rubbed against her like a lover. Lucky bastard.

"It, um, was a nice evening," she said finally. "How about for you?"

"Well, I was with Trevor at Max's, as you well know." I shot her a knowing look. "He brought a new friend back to his place, so I was left to my own devices for most of the night."

"What? *You* didn't bring home a new friend?"

"I did not," I told her, giving her the information straight. Let her judge me if she dared.

"So, no one caught your eye last night?"

I crossed my arms and grinned at her. "I wouldn't say that, Vicky."

She glanced up at me, startled but, clearly, not knowing how to respond. I'd been vague enough to keep her guessing. Score one point for me.

Winston fought to keep her attention on him. He jumped up on his hind legs and did a five-second jig, the little show off. But he got what he wanted. Vicky laughed and clapped and focused entirely on him. And when Winston returned to all fours again, she scratched behind his ears and said, "What a clever boy you are. Such a sweetheart, too!"

Shit. I was feeling jealous of my dog again. He was plainly smarter than me in winning over the French teacher's affection. That much was obvious. But, although Winston was cuter and a better dancer, I could do a few things he couldn't.

I pulled Winston's favorite chew toy—a stuffed white bunny—out of my pocket and threw it toward the center of the park. "Go fetch!" I said. "Go get the bunny!"

Winston took off like a shot, and I stepped closer to Vicky.

We both watched as he came bouncing back with the toy. I threw it again, farther this time. Off he went and, as expected, got distracted by a couple of squirrels. Eastman Field was usually full of them.

"He's absolutely adorable, Blake."

"Thanks, I know." I paused. "So, do I need to do a jig to get you to look at me like that?"

She chuckled, one of those slightly embarrassed laughs that happen when someone doesn't have a clue how to answer. I decided it was time to arm wrestle a response from her.

"I'm not the world's greatest dancer," I admitted, "but I know a few clubs in the city that have good music. Couples have been known to hit the dance floor there, too. Or just sit and listen to the tunes over drinks and appetizers."

"Hmm," she said noncommittally, her eyes still on my

dog, who was prancing around the middle of the mostly empty park, having the time of his furry life.

I tapped her shoulder to get those dark eyes of hers back on my face. "Okay, subtlety is not working for me here. Let me try this again." I took a deep breath. "Mademoiselle, I don't believe we got off on the right foot. So, I'd really like to take you out for an evening. On a proper date. With food and drinks and conversation and stuff like that."

"Why?"

"What do you mean—*why?* Because. Because...I like you. And you like my dog, which is *almost* like liking me. And I want to talk with you outside of your classroom or random meetings around town."

She eyed me with suspicion. "They're not entirely random. You've been following me."

"I haven't been 'following' you like some crazy stalker. What kind of a man do you think I am?"

She raised her brows, but there was a hint of a smile fighting to emerge at the corners of her mouth.

She was smart, so I had to play this candidly.

"All right, no. Don't answer that," I said. "I wasn't trailing you around Mirabelle Harbor, exactly, but I was kind of *hoping* we'd run into each other. Playing the odds on where I might see you, okay?"

The twitching of her lips finally turned into a bona fide smile. *Yes.* This wasn't a total win yet, but I was inching closer. I was wearing her down.

"You already asked me out, Blake, remember? Drinks and then going back to your place and getting naked? I clearly recall saying no to your offer."

I gave her my most charming grin. "We won't go back to my place—" *Not this first time, anyway...* "We'll just have the drinks and, maybe, order some dessert. Would you agree to that?"

There was a pause that lasted about three centuries.

"I—I'll think about it," she said, turning to gaze briefly at Winston, who was enthusiastically doing another goofy prancy dance, spinning in circles and trying either to regain our attention or impress the squirrels. I wasn't sure which.

I just knew that Vicky was finally—if marginally—warming up toward me. And Winston was definitely helping. For the briefest moment, I was filled with a sense of rightness and contentedness.

Pleased as I was with this situation, I began making mental plans for whatever might come next. We'd flirt some more. I'd flatter her a little. She'd see through my game, but I'd disarm her with my sense of humor. I'd make her laugh and, eventually, get her to nail down a date. I was *good* at this, and I knew Vicky and I would have some fun for however long it lasted.

So I was biding my time. Happy to stand where I was, feeling the sun warming my face. Vicky beside me. My dog playing nearby.

Then a group of runners jogged by us.

I laughed at first. They were like a flash mob, coming together from every corner of Eastman Field, as if they'd agreed to meet here at noon sharp and had invited everyone in their path to join in.

Winston, just a few yards away in his own doggy world, was startled by the sudden rush of people. I could hear his bark of panic as the runners flowed around us. I called out his name, but he was already spooked. Strangers, especially large crowds of them, always freaked him out.

But then one runner's foot connected with the toy bunny and sent it sailing toward the edge of the park. Winston's eyes followed it, barking in alarm and searching for anything familiar among the chaos.

Scared and unleashed, he bolted away from the pack of runners as soon as they cleared—dashing toward the toy, which had been kicked again, and straight into the parkway's traffic.

"NO!" I yelled, when I saw where he was running. Mirabelle Parkway was one of the busiest streets in the northern suburbs. "Winston come back!"

It happened in a split second. A devastating fracture of time.

I heard a honking car horn.

A shout.

A sickening thud.

I watched in horror as Winston's fluffy body flew through the air and landed in a heap against the curb.

I didn't have the breath to utter a word. My heart, my lungs, and my brain function stopped cold. I just sprinted toward him, praying for the first time since my mom's stroke that a living creature might miraculously live longer than expected.

My prayers counted for shit last time, but I was willing to try anything as I knelt beside my dog, gently cradling his head and checking for blood, broken bones, signs of life.

He was so small. Such a little body underneath all of that cream-colored fur. And he was knocked out cold. Paws so limp that he looked dead, although I could still feel warmth when I touched him.

In my head, I was screaming, but my mouth didn't work. And I couldn't think.

My pulse had frozen, too. Didn't know what to do to revive him. The devastation of losing Zeus those years ago flooded me all over again.

I was vaguely aware of cars whizzing by. A few had slowed down. One blue van screeched to a halt near us.

The driver, an older woman, shouted to us, asking if my dog was okay. She'd seen him get sideswiped by that fucking SUV. Wanted to know if we needed help.

I couldn't answer. Hell, I couldn't even move.

But Vicky, breathing hard beside me, spoke for us both. "We need to get him to the animal hospital. Now." She was smoothing Winston's brow. Concentrating hard on something. "He's alive, Blake," she said in an urgent voice. "Lift him up carefully, okay? Hold him against you, and try to keep his spine straight." As I did that, she pointed toward the vehicle belonging to the concerned woman who'd stopped for us. "Get in the van," Vicky commanded, "and let's go."

~*Vicky*~

It had been a long time since I'd seen anyone in a state of shock, but a person never forgot what it looked like.

No matter how much of a tough-guy façade Blake might put on, his silence in this situation wasn't a sign of strength. He was trembling and probably didn't even realize it. Completely disoriented, like a victim in the aftermath of a bombing.

The woman who'd stopped and picked us up had a pink-clad toddler in the backseat, strapped into a booster chair and staring at Blake and me with large blue eyes.

"Sleeping doggy?" the little girl asked Blake as he climbed into the backseat clutching Winston and muttering inarticulately under his breath.

"Yes," I told the child. Then I whispered to the girl's mother, "The emergency vet on Spring Street, please." She nodded and sped us there like a race car driver on the last lap.

"We can't thank you enough," I told her as Blake and I slid out of the van.

She thrust a business card at me. "Leave me a message and let me know how he is, okay?"

I nodded.

She lowered her voice. "Both the dog *and* your friend," she added with a worried look in Blake's direction.

"I will," I said. "Thank you."

Blake was already running through the doors of the animal hospital with Winston clutched to his chest. I ran after them just in time to hear Blake finally speak. "Please. Please help him," he said to the receptionist, sounding terrified. "He was hit by a car." Then to Winston in a hoarse whisper, "Hang in there, Buddy. I—I need you."

For the next hour and a half, Blake mostly paced around the waiting room, stopping only when there was news of some kind.

The two vets on call both examined Winston immediately and thoroughly, and they concluded he had a bad forelimb injury—a "brachial plexus avulsion," they called it—and most likely a serious concussion.

"It's the leg that must have hit the pavement first," said Jill, one of the vets.

I heard Blake swear under his breath.

"The good news," said Aidan, the other vet, "is that his leg isn't broken. It's a manageable injury. We're binding it, and we'll give him anti-inflammatory meds to reduce the swelling. Hopefully, with some care, it should heal in a couple of months."

Blake looked marginally relieved. "What about the concussion, though?"

Jill reached out and squeezed his arm, compassion softening her gaze. "We also took a CT scan of his brain to make sure there was no build up of blood or any other fluid in his head. Thankfully, we didn't see any severe damage, but head injuries are always tricky. We need to wait for Winston to wake up, and then we can run a few other tests."

Blake nodded, pacing miserably again the moment the vets were out of sight.

Periodically, one of them would emerge from the back and fill us in on something.

"When can I see him?" Blake asked a while later.

"Give us another half hour or so," the vet replied before heading back in.

I'd already asked Blake twice if he wanted some coffee

or a sandwich. He refused. But as the minutes wore on, I wondered if there was anything at all I could do for him that would help. He looked so helpless, so lost, so afraid. And, at the same time, he seemed almost resigned to the sadness. Like he'd been in this situation before and expected complications and an unhappy ending.

I knew how scary it could be when a beloved pet was sick or hurt. I'd been here once when Napoleon had eaten some tainted tuna. The manufacturers had recalled the batch, but not before hundreds of cats had fallen ill.

It was infuriating that some careless, speeding driver had caused Winston's injuries and hadn't even stopped to help. But we were here, now, getting him excellent treatment. He was alive. He'd be okay.

"They're taking good care of him," I whispered to Blake. "Winston's going to be all right. Don't worry."

He shook his head. "It's my fault. I shouldn't have taken him off his leash. I should have kept my eyes on him at all times. It's my fault," he repeated.

"It was an accident. If that crowd of runners hadn't spooked him or if his toy hadn't been bunted toward the street or if that driver had been going slower or paying more attention, Winston would have been fine."

"But I knew he could be skittish—"

"Blake, listen to me. I'm not saying what happened today was a good thing, but it could have been a lot worse. You know that. A dog can recover from an injured leg and even a bad concussion. And Winston *will*. He's strong enough to fight this and heal. He adores you. He wants to stay with you."

He was standing very still. If it hadn't been so quiet in the waiting room, I wouldn't have heard his shuddering intake of breath. If I hadn't been watching him so closely, I would have missed the wetness in his eyes that he blinked away.

He turned abruptly toward the coffee station, his back

to me, and cleared his throat. "Thanks, Vicky. Um, I'm gonna have some coffee now and just hang out here until they let me take him home. You've been great. Really, *really* great. But there's nothing either of us can do for Winston right now, and I'm sure you have other things to do with your day." He finally turned around, holding a cup of coffee that I doubted he had any intention of drinking. "You should get out of here. Do whatever you—"

"Don't be ridiculous," I said. "I'm staying."

Blake tried to talk me into going, but he was too shaken up to form a convincing argument, and I just flat out refused to leave.

"If anything like this ever happens to my cat, God forbid, you can spend the day at the vet with me, okay?" I said. "Napoleon and I have been together for six years. He's a member of my family. Just as Winston is a member of yours."

Blake set his unwanted coffee on the counter and smiled briefly for the first time in two hours. "Why am I not surprised that you named your pet after a French dictator?"

I smiled back just as the lady vet came out into the room. "Winston is conscious but very groggy. If you'd like to see him for a few minutes, you may. But it's best if we keep him here overnight for observation."

Blake's eyes widened. "I can't take him home?"

"Hopefully tomorrow," Jill said. She motioned him to follow her. "Why don't you both come back?"

I hung a few steps behind as we entered a small room with Winston atop a table, his head resting on a cushion. Blake rushed over to him and leaned in close.

"I'm so sorry," he whispered, his hands hovering above the dog's furry body, as if afraid to touch him and do any more damage. Blake finally stroked him around the bandaging, as gently as if he were caressing an infant.

Winston's eyes were heavy, but they opened when he

sensed his owner's presence, and he licked Blake's nose with his tiny pink tongue.

"Hey, little buddy." Blake bowed his head. I couldn't see his face, but his shoulders were shaking.

I stepped out of the room.

"I'm going to be back in about twenty or thirty minutes," I told the receptionist. "I'm sure Blake will still be here with Winston and might not even notice that I'm gone. But, in case he asks, please tell him I just ran out to get something."

"Of course," the woman said. "Glad Winston is going to be okay."

I nodded at her. "So am I," I said, shuddering at the thought of Blake's reaction if circumstances had been worse. Then I slipped outside and let myself cry tears both happy and sad. Tears for the dog who'd been hurt today...but who would recover. And tears for the man who wasn't quite the cocky, confident, devil-may-care bad boy he showed the world.

The Blake Michaelsen I'd seen this afternoon wasn't the same angry guy who'd gotten into a fistfight at Max's Pub. He wasn't the ultra-cool DJ who'd been so quippy on the radio. He wasn't even the irritating flirt who'd burst into my classroom, poked fun at me, and made a habit out of coming up with new indecent proposals.

No, this guy was a total stranger. A heartbreakingly vulnerable man who could be flattened by the fear of losing somebody. A man who claimed not to believe in love and, yet, had given his heart to a matted mess of a mutt he'd had for only a month.

Would the real Blake Michaelsen please stand up?

Whoever this stranger was, he was going to need transportation back to his home. And though I didn't know exactly where Blake lived, I doubted he'd be up for a walk, however long or short, after today's ordeal.

My apartment was only about twenty minutes away on

foot, and I could change out of my workout clothes, bring back my car and my ebook reader, and grab a few granola bars for the hours ahead. If Blake wasn't able to take Winston home tonight, he'd very likely be staying at the clinic for as long as the vets would let him.

When I returned to the animal hospital, the receptionist said Blake was still in the room with Winston, just as I'd expected. I thanked her and sat back down in the waiting room, flipped my e-reader open to the romance I was enjoying, and nibbled on a chocolate-oat-cranberry bar.

Blake emerged from the back about an hour later. "Vicky, you're still here... I'm sorry. I kinda lost track of time. I should have checked in with you sooner—" He paused. "You changed your outfit."

"I did, but I'm back. How's he doing?"

"Better. He's still feeling the effects of the local anesthesia for his leg. He'll be more alert when that wears off, but he'll feel his injuries more, too. I just want to be here for him."

"I know." I tossed a granola bar at him. "Eat something, Blake. Then go back and spend some more time with your dog. I'll be right here when you come out again."

He unwrapped the snack and took a bite. After he swallowed, he said, "I just realized I'm starving. Thank you."

"You're welcome. Now do you finally want a sandwich?"

He shook his head. He still looked serious and unsettled, but the deep pain and fear that had been etched upon his features right after the accident were fading. There was a little more color in his complexion. A bit more lightness in his eyes.

"They're gonna kick me out at six," he said. "You really don't have to stay. But, if you're crazy enough to still be here then, I'd like to buy you dinner. No music or dancing. No games or anything. Just food, okay? You've got to be starving, too."

I smiled at him. "Okay." I pointed at my vehicle, parked across the street. "I went and got my car. We can go to eat wherever you want."

He walked over to me and knelt down in front of my chair. "I have no idea how to thank you for everything you've done today."

I shrugged. "You don't have to. Just give Winston a hug from me. I'm so, so relieved that he's all right."

Blake stared at me for a long, silent moment. Then he took hold of my free hand and pressed his lips to my skin. I could still feel the potency of his touch, even a few moments later, after he'd disappeared into the back again.

By the time six p.m. came, I was only a few chapters away from finishing my novel. Another vet had come in for the nightshift and was appraised of what had been going on. She promised to keep a close eye on Winston, monitor him carefully throughout the night, and alert us if there were any worrisome changes.

"It's best for him to stay here for observation," the new vet said. "With a concussion like he had, if even the smallest issue arises, we don't want there to be a moment's delay in treatment."

"So get some rest, Blake," Aidan said. "You need it. You can come back tomorrow morning and, hopefully, take him home around noon."

After Blake thanked all of the vets and made a call to one of his bosses at the radio station, telling the guy that he needed to take the next day off, he finally let me lead him to my car. I could see the exhaustion of the day weighing on him. He wore it like a heavy woolen cloak.

"So, where to?" I asked. "Something ethnic? We've got Greek, Italian, Thai, and Mexican close by. Or there's seafood. Or burgers."

"Burgers," he said quickly. "At Sloppy Joe's. Please. That goes best with beer."

"I'm not sure how much beer you should be drinking, especially after hardly eating anything today."

"Believe me, I know," he said, as I pulled the car out into the road and headed toward one of Mirabelle Harbor's most popular hamburger joints. "That's why we're getting the food to go. We'll have the drinks afterwards."

"Where? I'm not going to a bar, Blake."

"Just try to trust me for fifteen minutes, okay?" He asked me how I liked my burgers, quizzed me on favorite side dishes, pulled out his cell phone, and called in an order that would feed about fourteen people.

We got to Sloppy Joe's and sat in the parking lot until our food was ready. He wasn't particularly chatty, but he made a handful of comments that let me know he was doing okay, all things considered.

"This is weird," he observed, glancing around the car. "I'm almost never in the passenger's seat."

"No one ever drives you anywhere?"

"One of my brothers. Sometimes. It's pretty rare."

"You're used to being in charge."

He nodded as if it had never occurred to him that it could be any other way.

Personally, I liked driving well enough, but I didn't love it. I didn't need to be the one behind the wheel to feel comfortable or in control. I sensed Blake felt differently, especially as he shifted uncomfortably in the seat next to me, ready to spring out of the car the second he thought he could pick up our order.

When he brought the food back, he gave me driving instructions that were pretty straightforward—"Take the first left up ahead. Left again at the stop sign..."—and soon we were in a parking lot to an apartment complex.

I'd foolishly assumed we were headed to a park or somewhere neutral, to make a picnic of it and eat our burgers outside. I thought he'd try to talk me into going to one of the bars in Harbor Square afterward, since I'd been driving in that general direction. But I suddenly realized he had a different dining and drinking plan altogether.

"Next time, I'd like to take you out for a real meal at a restaurant of your choice, Vicky. You've been nothing short of amazing today." He paused and looked at me until he was sure I'd heard him. "But the truth is that I'm not fit for being out in public right now. Even just picking up carryout at Sloppy Joe's, I ran into people I knew. And I don't feel like pretending tonight. I actually don't want to talk to anyone but you."

He pointed at the building next to us, a few floors up. "That's my place. Please come in. I promise you'll be safe. I just need to kick back, eat something, drink just a couple of beers, and try not to miss my dog too much. I don't know why you stuck around with me all day, but if you can tolerate me for a hour or two more, I'd love to have your company."

What could I say to that?

"All right," I said. But when Blake grinned like a naughty schoolboy who'd just gotten his way, I added, "Only because I'm really hungry. Try anything, and you'll regret it."

"Oh, Mademoiselle. I wouldn't dare."

Injured dog or no, I had a hard time believing there was much Blake Michaelsen wouldn't dare to do.

Up in his apartment, as he pulled out the stacks of food containers from the bag, I had the chance to glance around his place. I was, admittedly, pleasantly surprised by it. It wasn't fastidiously tidy or anything, but it was fairly neat, organized, and nicely decorated. It was also well stocked with books. Two *walls* of hardcovers and paperbacks on massive bookshelves. There was a huge flat-screen TV, too, but I also spotted a globe on the table next to it and a half dozen black-and-white framed photographs that featured famous landmarks from around the world. The Great Wall of China. The Egyptian Pyramids. The Roman

Colosseum. The Eiffel Tower.

"La Tour Eiffel," I murmured.

"Oui," he said. "I didn't take that picture, but I really like looking at it."

"So, you haven't been to France?"

"I wish." He handed me a plate with a hot burger on it—Swiss cheese dripping delectably down the bun—and then pointed to the gazillion side dishes on his countertop. "Eat something."

By this time, my stomach was rumbling, so I added a handful of fries, some salsa and guacamole, tortilla chips, and a couple of barbequed wings to my plate before digging in.

As soon as he started devouring his meal, I resumed the discussion. "Does that mean you'd like to go to Paris then?"

"I'd like to go everywhere," he replied in between bites of wings and fries. "London. Paris. Rome. Agra. Beijing. Khartoum. Sydney. Ulan Bator. Antanarivo."

"Antana-what?"

"The capital of Madagascar."

"Oh." Okay...wow. The guy knew his geography.

He winked at me, obviously pleased that he'd managed to surprise me. "Hey, what can I get you to drink?" He marched into the middle of the kitchen. "I've got cold beer, whisky, rum, tequila, vodka, orange juice, Coca Cola, and coffee."

"I'll just have one beer," I said, since he'd gotten me thinking about how good that would taste with our burgers.

"Beer is what I'm having, too," he said, pulling two chilled bottles out of the fridge. "But no one ever stops at one."

"I do."

He shot me a disbelieving look along with a grin. "Want a glass?"

I shook my head. "This is perfect, thank you." I twisted

the bottle open and took a sip. It was cold, bitter, good. An excellent pairing with the burger.

As he walked back toward me, his foot bumped against something and he halted, his smile disappearing. He picked up the object—a rawhide doggy treat—and slipped it inside a drawer. For a second, I could see the anguish and worry cross his face. But he just exhaled, opened his own beer, and downed about half of it before he spoke again.

"I know I keep saying this, but I really don't know what I would've done without you today, Vicky. Thanks for staying. Not just when we were at the vet for Winston, but here. Now." He raised his beer across the counter to meet mine, clinked bottles with me, and then finished the contents of his before returning to the fridge to grab another one.

"We don't have to eat at the counter," he added. "We can sit on the sofa, if you'd like. Watch something mindless on TV."

I didn't know what to say. I was still thinking about his interest in travel but wasn't sure what to ask next. So I transferred to the sofa and waited for inspiration.

Blake clicked on his huge TV and started flipping through cable stations. There was a baseball game in progress. A Comedy Central sketch. A teen movie with shapeshifters or something. A hot-n-heavy HBO drama where the main couple was uncomfortably going at it on top of a pool table.

I cringed. "Maybe not that."

He laughed. "That was my favorite option of the bunch," he said, but he immediately clicked off the TV. "We could stream a movie, if you'd like."

"I'm fine. I'd rather just talk with you."

He looked stunned. "Really?"

"Yeah, really." I pointed at the globe and a few of the other landmark photographs. "Tell me more about all of these."

He shifted in his seat with a squirm of uneasiness. I wondered why asking about these items would be awkward. Was travel a sensitive subject? Or photography?

He swallowed and said, "These are all places I'd hoped to get to visit by now. I've got a passport. Just haven't had the chance to put it to use yet."

I nodded. "Traveling can be really expensive."

"Yeah," he agreed. "And dangerous."

"Depending on where you go, sure."

He half smiled at me. "That's true, too, but that wasn't the kind of danger I was talking about." He took a big bite out of his burger, chewing slowly and thoughtfully before continuing. "There's also what you leave behind here at home. The danger that it won't still be there when you return."

I squinted at him. "Did a girlfriend of yours break up with you after a trip or something?"

The corners of his eyes crinkled in amusement. "Oh, definitely. I've had girlfriends break up with me for all kinds of reasons. They wouldn't even have to leave the country. One broke up with me after just taking a trip to the mall."

"No, she didn't."

He laughed. "She totally did. She said that when she realized she was more excited about buying socks at the mall than about our date that night, she knew we didn't belong together."

"That's crazy," I said. But it was also funny. Blake exuded energy. And sex appeal. And mischief. Although he would probably make a very difficult boyfriend for a lot of women (me included), I couldn't imagine anyone preferring sock shopping to an evening out with him. That was ludicrous.

He shrugged in a cute, self-deprecating way. "But it's the truth, Vicky." He was working on his second beer. He caught me staring at his bottle. "Need another one yet?"

"I'm only halfway through this one," I informed him. "And when I've finished it, I'm heading home."

He scowled at me. "You can't leave so soon. I have questions for *you*."

"Oh?"

"Yeah. I wanna know where you've traveled. France, right? Belgium? Switzerland?"

I nodded. "Yes, to all three." I didn't want to mention that Philippe's family was originally from Brussels, or that he had been on that trip with me, so I conveniently left out that part. But I told Blake about the one Grand European adventure I'd had a few years ago. "I was in England, Germany, Austria, and Italy, too. It was a tour that lasted almost a month—beginning in London and ending in Rome. I started saving for it as soon as I began teaching, and it was worth every penny."

"Must have been incredible," he said wistfully. Then he added, "Wait. You studied to be a French teacher before you'd ever been to France?"

I'd been asked this scores of times during college and my early teaching years. Usually, it made me feel a bit defensive, but I could tell Blake's question wasn't out of rudeness. Just pure curiosity.

"I took a couple of trips to Quebec," I explained. "Once in high school, which was when I first fell in love with the language. And once in college, as part of a study abroad program for French majors. It's a gorgeous place. Easily my favorite part of Canada. It's so European in architecture and attitude. But it's been nine years since I was last there. I'd love to go back."

"Sounds wonderful," he said, finishing his second beer and eyeing the fridge. Would he get another one so soon?

But he didn't stand up—for more beer or for any other reason. He seemed lost in thought. Maybe thinking about lands left unexplored or, catching sight of another of his dog's toys, thinking again about Winston.

In any case, Blake looked serious, and I wanted to try to lighten his mood, so I thought of a new subject.

"What do you enjoy most about being a radio DJ?" I asked.

Oooh. Bad choice.

His expression turned from serious to almost...angry. But why? He jumped up and headed into the kitchen portion of the apartment before I could figure it out. Across the large room, I could see him pouring himself something. Was it a different kind of alcohol?

No, I realized with relief. It was just a cola this time. So he *could* stop after two beers—just as he'd said. That was encouraging.

He returned to the living room area before even attempting to answer my DJ question. When he did start talking, though, what came out of his mouth was nothing short of a tirade.

I actually couldn't understand what he was saying at first. It was all ranting and infuriated mumbling. But he finally spoke loudly enough for me to catch some of his commentary.

"It wouldn't be so bad if it weren't for society's slavish devotion to tedious and uninspiring musical groups that are one-hit wonders...or should be. And don't even get me started on soloists like Barry Connelly," he warned.

"I like Barry Connelly."

He shook his head, as if trying to dislodge my words from his brain, and muttered some more. Then he took a few gulps of his soda before finally saying, "Yeah, you, my sister, and about half of the Chicagoland listening area should form a fan club."

This was clearly a sore subject. I tried to salvage the conversation by twisting it in yet another direction.

"So, all right. What if you weren't a DJ? What would you being doing instead?"

He crossed his arms and pondered this for a

surprisingly long time. "You want to know the truth, Vicky?"

"I *always* want to know the truth, Blake."

He grinned. "Okay. Truth is, I actually love being a DJ. I don't always agree with the music on rotation at 102.5, but the job itself suits me. It's nothing but cool. And the people at the station aren't half bad." He shrugged, like it cost him something to admit this.

"Is that why you're still working there, even though you don't like love songs?"

He nodded. "I mean, some of the songs aren't *terrible*. I just think they're really overrated. And others...well, a few of them make my ears bleed."

"So, what music do you really like then?" I pointed at the iPod resting in its dock on one of his bookshelves. "Would you play me something you love?"

He squinted at me, considering, then walked over to his iPod and fiddled with it. A moment later, the opening strains of an early Air Supply song—"Lost in Love"— came on. He was bobbing his head along with it, deep in thought.

I laughed. "You're kidding me. All that talk about hating romance and you choose *this?*"

He stopped bobbing his head and shot me a demonic grin. "I *am* kidding. Shar downloaded this onto my device a few months back when I had it connected to my computer, just to piss me off. I keep meaning to delete it, but—" He paused, a mischievous look crossing his face. "Sometimes it has its uses."

"Ah, I get it. Part of your Seduction Playlist, right?"

"You know me better than I thought." He scrolled through a bunch of other songs before clicking on one. The tune started with piano and built to a crescendo with guitars and drums. The lyrics were thoughtful and, admittedly, more poetic than I would have expected. But I knew this wasn't one of Blake's joke songs. He really loved this one.

"It's good," I said after listening to the first verse and the chorus. "What's the title?"

"It's called 'Superheroes.' Came out a few years ago by an Irish band called The Script."

The group's name sounded familiar to me, although I wouldn't be able to list any of their songs. "What else do you like?" I asked.

"Hmm." He played me a snippets of songs by a variety of musical artists: "Second Chance" by Shinedown, "If Today Was Your Last Day" by Nickelback, "Strength" by The Alarm, "Real World" by Matchbox Twenty. And there were more—recent releases by bands I couldn't identify, older groups that I didn't know well—but I was recognizing a theme running between all of his choices. The songs Blake liked best were about finding the inner strength to do something extraordinary. Not about the love of another person, but more about the need to tap into one's personal power and finally be able to come into one's own. That made sense to me. A prerequisite for being able to love someone else was, after all, the capability to love oneself. And, perhaps, Blake wasn't quite there yet.

When the Bon Jovi song "It's My Life" came on, he was still standing halfway across the room, arms crossed, gazing at me with an uncomfortable expression, as if he'd guessed that I was trying read him. Trying to figure out something personal, secretive, significant about him. Something he wasn't inclined to let most people know.

But he'd been more real with me today than he'd ever been, and I more than suspected that few humans outside of his family got a glimpse into Blake Michaelsen with his social mask off.

But it would be a lie to say that his naked gaze wasn't unsettling to me. As much as I was trying to get some insight into him, he was studying me just as closely. Reading my reactions to his songs. Coming to conclusions.

I took one last sip of my beer and figured it was well

past time to go.

He finished his soda in one gulp, set the glass down near his iPod, and came over to me just as I stood to leave.

"Thanks for dinner, Blake."

He shook his head. "You can't leave yet. You've still got beer in that bottle." He smiled this lopsided grin at me, like a little kid.

"I know when I've had enough."

He covered his heart with his palm, comically. "Are you trying to wound me?"

I laughed and shook my head. "Definitely not. But my tolerance for alcohol isn't nearly as well developed as yours." I didn't know what it was about Blake. He was only a few months older than me, but I felt so young and inexperienced around him. Like a teenager at her first big party.

"You *are* a lightweight," he agreed, eyeing my body as if he were scanning it. His gaze didn't miss a centimeter. Then, he took a step forward.

I took a step back.

He chuckled. "Don't worry, I'm going to let you go. Just allow me to walk you to your car, okay?"

"Thanks." I grabbed my purse and my keys. We got as far as his apartment door when I turned to face him. "Please let me know how Winston is doing tomorrow. I'm hoping he'll be running around and bouncing up on people in no time."

"Me, too. Thank you again for everything, Vicky."

I put my hand on the doorknob and he put his hand over mine. It was like the zing of an electric shock but without the pain. His touch singed my skin with heat, but I couldn't bring myself to pull away.

Blake reached out to hug me and, again, I was powerless. I couldn't push him back. Not when he enfolded me into an embrace that was warmer and more sensual than I'd ever experienced. And more passionate than I could have imagined.

Gratitude could do that, though. He was feeling very thankful for my help. That was all.

And I almost succeeded in believing it, too, except...when we finally separated after the hug, he looked me in the eye and whispered my name. Then he drew me close to him again, so our bodies were flush, and I could feel the tension and the wanting in every place where we connected.

The iPod was still playing, moving between songs without Blake directing it and filling the room with music. It was a rap-like tune that I couldn't identify, but the lyrics involved having a "reason to remember the name." All I could think was "Blake Michaelsen. Blake Michaelsen." His was a name I could hardly forget.

Although, when he brought his lips down to meet mine, I nearly forgot my *own* name.

Whoa. The boy knew how to kiss.

A small voice in my head screamed, "That's because he's so well practiced!" But the rest of me...just...just let go.

His hands encircled my hips and his mouth consumed mine. The heat coming from his mouth, his lips, his tongue—it was like breathing in fire. And it was *scorching*. A bone-deep, dry flame that burned on contact. There was no doubt that I'd lost all sense of autonomy. That I belonged to him in this moment. Completely.

And there was something else. After reading romance novels for a couple of decades, I finally understood what the writers meant when the heroine felt like she was floating. I'd never experienced that kind of weightlessness. I was levitating and burning up at the same time. A rising fireball that only became more incendiary when Blake pressed me against his door, and I could fully feel his body's response to mine.

"God, Vicky, I want you," he murmured, as he crushed

my chest with his and ran his tongue along the side of my neck.

Every one of my senses wanted to float higher, burn faster.

But my mind had begun processing his words. Analyzing them. And my fingertips started cooling. My feet started sinking, slowly, back to the floor.

"You had a rough day," I managed to say. "You're drained emotionally. And you're vulnerable."

"So?" One of his hands lifted the hem of my shirt and slipped between the fabric and my skin, caressing the area just above my waistband. I almost moaned.

"You need comfort and company," I reasoned. "You don't really want *me* tonight."

"Oh, yes. I do." He nipped at my earlobe and the pleasure jettisoned out to every possible nerve ending in my body.

I shook my head and pulled back a few millimeters, just enough to create a little distance. "No, Blake. You just want *somebody*. That's a different thing."

He stopped kissing and caressing me and just stared. "Not true. What do I have to do to convince you?"

I smiled. "This isn't a persuasive speech for class or some kind of debate-team competition. Besides, you already told me how you feel about 'love.' It's a sham. Something fake. A combination of lust plus obsessiveness plus dependency. I—I like you, Blake. A lot more than I'd expected to, actually. But I can't be part of an equation like that."

He pulled away from me as if I'd zapped him with an electrical wire, and then ran his fingers through his dark hair. "I'd tell you almost anything to get you to stay," he replied softly. "But I won't go back on what I said about love. It's a self-delusion for people who wander through life with those freakin' clichéd rose-colored glasses. Another cliché, and a more realistic one, is that life's a bitch and then you die. There's no long-term happily ever after. I wish I didn't believe that, but I do."

I winced. I hated the pessimism of statements like that. Just because I hadn't found my true love story yet, that didn't mean it didn't exist. And unlike Blake, I needed to believe it did.

"But," he continued, "two people can still find pleasure in each other. Sometimes. Like right here. Right now."

"You need to save hookup lines like that for someone who's a whole lot less self-delusional than me."

Blake sighed, a sound of resignation. "Damn. I was hoping it would work."

"Yeah, I know. Not that you aren't really tempting," I admitted, finally managing to open the door. "I can walk myself to my car. You'd better stay here and..." I eyed his body, all the signs of arousal still evident and obvious. "And, well, maybe, cool down a little."

"Are you suggesting I need a cold shower, Mademoiselle?"

I couldn't help but grin. "If that'll help."

He leaned in close and lowered his voice. "Only if you'll take one with me."

I rolled my eyes and escaped the building before my own desires could overrule my brain. But it was impossible to stop imagining that scenario on the drive home. And all night long. In vivid high definition and with crystal-clear surround sound.

More powerfully than any book hero or BBC film drama—classic or modern—Blake Michaelsen suddenly became my new romantic Dream Man.

However unlikely that was.

And however foolish I knew it to be.

CHAPTER NINE

~*Blake*~

The vets released Winston to my care Monday afternoon. He was swaddled in a binding, scraped, bruised, and needy, but so damn happy to see me that he wagged his tail, even though it had to hurt.

Couldn't stop holding him, stroking him, reassuring him that I was there. But something—or, rather, someone—was sharing my headspace. I couldn't look at my dog without also seeing Vicky in my mind's eye. The two were now linked because of this past weekend.

She was amazing.

An incredible, caring, intelligent woman.

And oh, my lord. *That kiss.* It was smokin'.

Problem was, because of the whole thing with Winston yesterday, I couldn't just disconnect from her. Compartmentalize my attraction to her from the woman herself, the way I would with some other chick. I'd always thought she was pretty, but that wasn't the only thing my brain was saying when she was in my arms. I wanted to sleep with her, sure, but I also wanted to talk with her and listen to her laugh and watch her react to things. Food she liked. TV shows she didn't. It was bizarre.

We weren't much alike, but I knew enough about opposites attracting not to be shocked that it could happen. I just never thought it could happen to *me*.

My kid brother Chance had been blindsided by this same thing earlier this year when he met Nia. Never much of an experimental eater (an understatement—the guy was a total health food freak who rarely strayed from his lean protein and fresh, unprocessed produce), Chance was now eating unpronounceable Greek dishes from Nia's family restaurant, and he even had an occasional dessert.

As for Nia, who'd had a lifelong aversion to fitness clubs, she was now working out regularly at Chance's gym and even running a 5K with my brother next month. Some kind of fall "Fun Run"—a form of weekend entertainment that I strained to wrap my mind around. The two of them would no doubt cross the finish line holding hands and celebrating with granola bars and bottled water. Nauseatingly sweet and wholesome but, I had to admit, there had been compromise on both sides. And I'd never seen my brother look so happy.

I pulled out my phone. I'd wrangled Vicky's cell number away from her during the evening. She'd asked me to let her know how my dog was doing, so it was time I made good on my promise to text her today. Plus, I couldn't get the woman out of my freakin' mind.

I adjusted a sleepy Winston on my leg. "Hey, buddy, wanna help me text the hot French teacher?" I asked him.

Winston opened his big eyes wide and gazed up at my face. Poor bastard was still so exhausted, he could barely raise his head.

"I'm talking about Vicky," I continued. "The lovely Mademoiselle."

This clarification seemed to help. Winston recognized that name and wagged his tail encouragingly.

My mutt was a chick magnet. Thanks to Winston, I'd met plenty of cute ladies on our walks around town. But he'd never taken to any of them as readily as he had to Vicky. And, obviously, neither had I. Like doggy, like owner.

"Hey, let me snap a quick picture of you. She thinks you're 'absolutely adorable.' And she was asking about you a lot. She wants to know how you're doing."

Gently, I positioned Winston on the sofa, bandaged front leg visible but not too traumatic looking, and then snapped the picture. I rubbed his head. "Okay. Now, what should I say?"

My dog didn't reply at first, he just sighed and sank deeper into the comfy black leather.

"All right, that's not a bad idea. I'll start with that. 'Winston is home and he's relaxing quietly on the sofa,'" I texted. "'We both are grateful to you for being there for us yesterday.' How does that sound?" I said, reading it aloud to Winston.

He barked.

"If it's good for you, it's good for me," I told him and clicked SEND. Then I blew a kiss at the phone screen.

To be honest, I hadn't expected an immediate response from her. It was nearing the end of the school day, and I knew Vicky had to be busy with her students.

So when I heard the ping a few moments later and saw her name pop up, I exclaimed, "Whoa!" so loudly that I startled my dog. "Miss Vicky just texted us back," I informed him. "I'll read it to you. She writes, 'So relieved to hear that, Blake! Thanks for letting me know. I've been so worried about him. And about you, too. Glad to hear all is well. And please give Winston a hug from me!' Hey, you get a hug, buddy." I gave him a careful squeeze. "That's from Vicky."

Winston looked duly impressed by this. I, however, was mildly miffed that he got a hug from her and I didn't.

So, I texted: "Winston liked his hug. Where's mine?"

The wait for a reply was longer this time, but I grinned like a kid at Christmas when I saw it pop up.

"Tell Winston to give you a hug for me."

"Just a hug?" I shot back.

"Well, yeah," she texted. "Unless, of course, you have a very different relationship with your dog than I realized..."

I hooted with laughter, which resulted in Winston looking at me with concern. "It's all good," I told him. "She's joking with us. That's an excellent sign." Then, to Vicky, I sent back an emoji that had a smiley face laughing so hard there were tears in its eyes.

"Fine," I texted after that. "Just a hug. For now. But when can you come over to visit us?"

"Not tonight, unfortunately. Staff meeting and about three hours of grading French essays. Can't tomorrow either. Student production of *The Mikado* that I promised to attend."

A Gilbert and Sullivan musical? I shuddered. I knew better, though, than to diss it. She loved all of those artsy things. "How about Wednesday?"

"Maybe."

Maybe wouldn't do. It was already going to be over forty-eight hours before I'd get to see her again, at the earliest. No way could I wait any longer than that.

I glanced around the apartment until I had a brainstorm. Grabbed a sheet of blank white copy paper and a black marker. In block letters, I printed: "Please come see me after school, Miss Vicky. I miss you. Love, Winston." I propped the page next to his sweet face and snapped another picture. Sent that to her.

My heart pounded as I waited for her to reply. It was, maybe, five minutes, but it felt like hours.

Then, finally: "You twisted my arm, Winston. I'll be there on Wednesday around four-thirty. Just for a quick visit, though. This is a busy time because we're prepping for Homecoming next week."

Shit. Homecoming.

I'd almost forgotten about that. Was it next week already? My required interactions with the lovely Mademoiselle were winding down too fast. I'd have to figure out my next move before next Friday night, or I wouldn't have a natural excuse to see her again.

Plus, I wanted to continue that kiss where we'd left off.

She might try to resist, but she'd been as into it as I was. I knew this for a fact. Those soft moans of hers gave it away. So did the flushed skin. The jackrabbit speed of her pulse. And the dark desire in her eyes. She was fighting it, but I knew women and their nonverbal signals. Vicky wanted me, too.

"Looking forward to seeing you" was all I texted. No way could I tell her just how much, though.

The next couple of days were a blur of work at the radio station, staying home as much as possible to take care of Winston, and daydreaming about the French teacher.

I was on familiar ground when it came to fantasies involving sexy ladies. I imagined us doing it everywhere and on every surface in my apartment, dark corners of the radio station, and locked rooms in public places. I'd traveled this mental playground before with countless bar babes that I'd been infatuated with for a week or two...so, briefly, it helped me keep Vicky at an emotional distance. It was just another crush.

But the second she walked through my door again on Wednesday afternoon, I was flooded with how different she was from the other women I'd fantasized about over the years.

Her scent was so deliciously her own. Fresh, floral, like

a garden on a bright summer morning.

Her voice was distinctive and so sweet. I desperately wanted to hear her call out my name.

Her eyes, chest, legs, thumbs, earlobes—damn. I wanted to touch every single part of her. My fingertips itched with it. I had to immediately snatch a beer from the fridge to keep myself from reaching out and grabbing her.

"Want something?" I asked, holding up a beer bottle in one hand and a can of soda in the other.

"Not this time. I can only stay for a half hour." She bent down to where Winston sat on the carpeted living room floor and lavished him with attention. He practically purred like a feline. Couldn't blame him. I would've purred, too, if she were stroking me like that.

"Look at you," she whispered to my dog. "You look so much better than you did on Sunday, you big sweetie." Then, to me, she added, "I left a message for that saint of a woman who drove us to the animal hospital. She'd asked me to let her know." Then, back to Winston, Vicky said, "Lots of people were worried about you."

As I watched the two of them together, I felt something peculiar and unfamiliar in my chest. Maybe this was a medical condition. Some sort of irregular heartbeat that my doctors had overlooked in past years. Or a new health problem that had recently developed. But something was definitely off. I couldn't seem to move. And my breathing was screwed up, too. It was tight. Shallow. I couldn't quite get enough air. What the hell?

I set both unopened beverages on the counter and finally regained the use of my legs. They were making a beeline toward her—my body acting before I could consciously decide to do anything. Being near Vicky, having her in my arms again, seemed to be the only way to relieve the odd tension in my chest. I just couldn't take it anymore.

I pulled her to standing, encircled her with as much of

myself as I could manage, and pressed my lips softly to her neck.

It helped, but the tightness squeezing my heart and lungs was still there.

"Blake," she whispered, but she didn't push me away. She wasn't resisting at all. In fact, her fingertips were digging into my back, pulling me closer, and her upper thighs were brushing against mine. I wanted to strip off her sturdy school clothes to get to the silky fabric underneath. But the second my fingers connected with the lacy waistband of her panties, I knew that was a lie.

I didn't give a damn about the delicate underwear. It was really only her skin that I wanted to touch.

I unbuttoned her black dress slacks, eased down the zipper, and got as far as sliding both the slacks and the panties halfway down her hips before her hands stilled mine.

"Blake," she said again, only this time it was a warning, not a breathless whisper.

"Vicky," I said back, mimicking her tone and using my free hand to shimmy up under her shirt until I reached her bra and could cup her breast in my palm. "You're wearing too many clothes."

"Yeah," she said, swallowing hard and putting one of her hands on top of my hand on her breast. The other hand shackled the wrist of my hand on her hip. "That's because I need to leave."

"Why?"

"Parent/teacher conferences are coming up in two weeks," she said sensibly, as if everyone on the planet knew this. "I need to get mid-semester grades turned in by this Friday."

I groaned and, with great reluctance, pulled away. "That means you'll be free on Friday night, right?"

She sighed. "Look, you're a very, very attractive man, Blake, but—"

"Oh, no. Stop right there while I'm ahead. You can't start a sentence so promisingly and then qualify it with a 'but.' I don't want any excuses, Mademoiselle. I owe you a real dinner out—the location of which you can choose, or I can choose. And it can be this Friday night, this Saturday night, or even this Sunday, but I *am* taking you out and I'm not taking no for an answer. Isn't that right, Winston?"

And perfectly on cue, my brilliant mutt barked.

In spite of herself, the serious Miss Vicky laughed. "You don't need to—"

"Yes, I do. Were you not listening to my last statement? Maybe this'll help." I pulled a slip of paper out of my pocket. "My cheat sheet," I admitted. I'd Googled the exact phrase so I could ask her to go out on the town with me this weekend in proper French. *"Je tiens à vous emmener sur en ville ce week-end. Dis oui, s'il vous plaît."*

I felt like I was waiting a decade before she finally responded.

"Oui," she said, while stepping back, re-zipping and re-buttoning her slacks, and straightening her shirt. She licked her lips, and they looked so kissable that I had to force myself not to pin her to the wall and devour her mouth.

I *needed* to sleep with her. That was the only chance I had to get this woman out of my system. The only cure in my arsenal of remedies. I knew from years and years of experience that nothing killed the flame of fantasy like the morning after a good, mindless roll in the sack. Until then, though, I'd be stuck daydreaming about her constantly and, even worse, imagining hanging out with her beyond our time in bed together. *That* was the most disturbing part. Vicky Bernier was beautiful, smart, and kind. Didn't matter how incredible she was, though, I didn't do long-term relationships. These insane feelings *had* to stop. And I knew how to stop them.

Once she and I slept together and faced the awkwardness (or indifference) that always followed, I wouldn't be a prisoner of these unsettling impulses any longer. And I'd bet anything that the weird tension in my chest would disappear, too. These were symptoms of an uncharacteristically deep infatuation—that was all.

"Excellent," I told her. "What night? What place? What time?"

"Saturday. You can choose the spot. Anytime after six."

I grinned. "It's a date. I'll pick you up at your apartment. Just text me the address...and be ready at 6:01."

CHAPTER TEN

~*Vicky*~

I'd been actively avoiding Shar all week.

Friday night, the Quest group was meeting for dessert at The Apple Factory in nearby Glen Forest for spiced apple cider, warm fritters, and slices of pie. I feigned exhaustion and, this time, I wasn't going to let Blake's sister talk me into going.

"Sorry," I told her. "I really can't come. With midterm grades due today and Homecoming Week starting this Sunday, I'm booked."

"But—" Shar protested.

"I'll be at the next gathering," I assured her, although, I suspected this might turn out to be untrue. Sharlene Michaelsen Boyd was an expert at reading other people's micro-expressions. She'd take one look at my face and just *know* that I'd been kissing her brother.

I did not need perceptive people around me this week. Especially not the day before a big date with Blake. And no matter how well—or how poorly—it went, one thing was absolutely certain: A relationship with him wouldn't last long.

But, hopefully, he had enough of a sense of self-preservation not to spill too many details about us to his overly curious little sister. For one thing, Shar would glom onto every bit of info like Krazy Glue and never forget a single word. And, for another, we both cared about her. I wouldn't want her to get caught in the middle of the fallout when everything flew to pieces.

And it would.

It was just a matter of how soon and if I'd be smart enough to step away the second I was capable of resisting Blake.

Unfortunately, this didn't seem to be possible when I was within ten feet of the guy.

Every ounce of good sense in my body dissipated into a wisp of air when he gazed at me with those mischievous dark eyes. Or when he said my name with his sexy DJ voice. Or, worst of all, when he caressed my skin with his fingertips, which were warm and slightly callused and very capable.

I shivered. I'd never wanted anyone to touch me as much as I wanted Blake to touch me. And, yet, how could that possibly end well? He didn't believe in love. Not that I could only date men who were serious about getting married, but what was the point in going out with somebody for whom a committed relationship wasn't even an option?

Nevertheless, when Blake appeared at my apartment door to pick me up on Saturday night—promptly at 6:01—I didn't turn him away.

"Wow. Punctual," I said instead, trying not to stare at him. Royal blue dress shirt. Dark jeans. So hot I could almost hear him sizzling.

"I'm a man of my word," he replied, stepping through the doorway and glancing around, taking in my small place with an alert and very interested gaze. "So," he added, "where's the little dictator?"

"Napoleon? He usually goes into hiding when visitors arrive. Probably lurking behind the sofa." I pointed to the middle of the living room and, sure enough, I spotted the distinctive swish of a gray tail at one end. I motioned Blake into the kitchen area a few feet away. "This might get him to show himself." I noisily opened a can of cat food and spooned it into Napoleon's bowl.

My cat slunk out from behind the furniture and regally strolled into the kitchen, as though he knew he was on parade. He eyed Blake suspiciously. As for me, he regarded me with his usual bored familiarity before digging into his dinner.

"That's about all the attention you can expect from him for now," I told Blake.

He chuckled. "He's a beautiful creature. Maybe I'll have better luck with him later."

"Maybe," I said, but I wasn't yet prepared to have Blake come back into my apartment after our date. There wasn't going to be a "later." Not if I knew what was good for me.

Already I could see Blake's gaze cutting curiously toward my bedroom door.

"Gonna show me around?" he asked.

I raised my eyebrows at him.

"Just a quick tour," he said, sounding amused, albeit slightly defensive. "I'm just trying to picture your surroundings."

"Fine." I had a one-bedroom apartment. This wouldn't take long.

We were already in the kitchen, so we walked a few steps and I let him get a full view of my living room. The TV and DVDs. My music and books. I had a few framed pictures of my parents. "I'm an only child," I said when he asked about siblings. He took in every item, including a handful of my French souvenirs. A glass bottle in the shape of the Eiffel Tower. A porcelain doll wearing a beret that I got in Paris.

"Cute," he said, playing with one of the dark curls on the doll's head, making it spring. Then he saw my e-reader on the end table. "May I take a look?"

"Sure. No romance bashing this time, though."

He clicked it on and it opened to a story I'd recently downloaded. It was the first in a multi-part romantic serial called *Alternate Austen*, and Part One was entitled "Pride, Prejudice, and Parallel Universes."

Blake squinted at the electronic text. He started reading aloud:

> *It is a truth universally acknowledged, that a single man in possession of a good intergalactic transportation device, must be in want of an interstellar mission.*

He grinned. "Seriously?"

"It's fiction, Blake. Fun, romantic Austen-inspired fiction."

He continued reading aloud in his skilled and devilishly sexy radio voice:

> *Captain James Fitzwilliam, commanding officer of the Starship Pemberley, turned to his second in command, Leonard Charles, and barked out his twenty-sixth order in half as many minutes.*
>
> *"Activate the cloaking device and set us on course eighty degrees due west toward Alpha Centauri," Fitzwilliam said. "We've gotten a report from Federation Headquarters of a disturbance near the Brighton-Hunsford System."*
>
> *Charles checked the graphics on his*

screen and frowned. "There's a documented black hole in the region, Captain. We're going to need to steer clear of the center and set our coordinates off to the northeastern side to avoid being drawn into its dark mass."

"We're at warp factor 9.2, Captain," Officer Radcliffe said. "If we maintain our course and speed, our expected arrival at the black hole will be in under an hour. But the televiewer is picking up an odd imbalance in the force field already," he admitted. "It's a separate entity from the black hole, however. And it's unlike anything we have on record, even utilizing the most updated intergalactic maps."

"A second black hole, perhaps?" Charles suggested.

Fitzwilliam shook his head. "It's behaving differently. Note the fluctuations on the oscelloscope. Not a black hole but—"

The rest of his words were lost in a vacuum as the entire vessel was sucked into something. A funnel? A shoot? To Fitzwilliam it felt like an amusement park ride, but without the safeguards. No rails. No brakes. No gravity.

Everyone on the starship screamed.

The Captain, grabbing onto his chair on the bridge, called out to his second, finishing his thought at last. "A wormhole."

"Where will we end up?" Charles called back.

"Who the bloody hell knows," retorted the Captain, seconds before everything went dark.

"Scene break," Blake said. Then, "I have no idea what the hell I just read, but it was damned funny." He closed my e-reader, set it back down on the table, and sauntered back toward me. "So, *Star Trek* meets Jane Austen, huh? I like sci-fi."

I shrugged. "You probably wouldn't like this. There's romance and kissing scenes and stuff."

"I got nothing against kissing scenes, Vicky. What happens next?"

"The members of the starship fall into a time warp and end up in a parallel literary universe. While caught in this new dimension, the Captain and his first officer are mistaken for Mr. Darcy and Mr. Bingley from *Pride and Prejudice* by two of the planet's inhabitants—Elizabeth and Jane Bennet—who've materialized from the pages of the Austen novel. The men need to decide if they'll stay in the parallel universe or if they'll try to reverse the warp and make their way home again."

"Odd but intriguing. I might just have to read more of this story later."

Once again, he was talking about "later." Wasn't going to happen.

Just. Say. No.

But what I said was, "Are you done being nosy now?"

"You still haven't shown me your bedroom." He grinned demonically.

"Yeah, we'll be saving that for 'later.'" I used air quotes.

"Oooh. You don't want me to come back up here, eh? Bet I can get you to change your mind."

I picked up my purse and my keys, strode to the door, and crossed my arms. "Don't push it."

He laughed and followed me out without a second's hesitation. I didn't know how to interpret that. Whether he'd decided to give me a break and drop it...or whether he was just so confident that he didn't bother to argue.

As I locked the door, he stared at me so hard, though, that I finally said, "What?"

"I neglected to tell you that you look stunning." He leaned in and kissed me very lightly on my cheek. "Thanks for going out with me tonight, Vicky. Hope you'll have fun."

As was the case before, wherever his lips touched my skin, I could feel a tingling. A wanting that spread from my face throughout my entire body. I stood paralyzed in the hallway, knowing with a certainty that was powerful and unerring that a night in bed with Blake Michaelsen would be pure pleasure. I had to do a better job of fighting that realization.

He was still staring at me, a knowing and sensual smile curling his lips upward. He could see right through me. But all he said was, "Shall we go?"

I nodded.

We must have been on the road for ten minutes before I managed to untangle my tongue and ask where we were headed.

"First, to dinner at a sweet Italian restaurant downtown. It's called La Bella Villa. Then to one of Chicago's dance clubs. It's small, intimate," he informed me. "The Crypt. Ever been there?"

I shook my head. "No. To both."

"Good. Then tonight will be all new."

I almost laughed. Tonight was going to be all new even if we just got burgers and fries from Sloppy Joe's again. Every moment I spent alone with Blake felt like I was traipsing over new territory. And there was something very different in the air between us tonight than there had been on Sunday back at his place. I didn't need the crew of the Starship Pemberley to tell me that I was on the edge of a major space-time disturbance, and I'd very likely get sucked into something highly dangerous and entirely unknown.

At the restaurant, Blake recommended the chicken marsala and the Italian sausage lasagna.

"Hard to choose between those," I said, although my stomach was flipping wildly. Wasn't sure how much I'd be able to eat of either dish.

"We could get one of each and split them," he suggested.

"Perfect."

Then he grinned at me again. Another one of his toe-curling smiles that made me feel as if I were back in high school in that empty gym with Jeremy Reede, the hottest guy in the sophomore class.

Jeremy was predatory with women—like Blake. Used to getting his way. Someone who knew the effect of his face and his expressions on others. The Charm Meister of Indiana's Cedar Grove High School District 127. And, for one quarter of that school year, I was his prey.

What I felt then mirrored almost exactly what I was feeling now. I was out of my depth and on the verge of drowning, but I was still frantically treading water anyway.

"You don't need to look so scared, Vicky," Blake said after the waiter brought us our meal. "You're not trapped here. If you don't like the food, we can leave."

"It's not the food," I murmured. Both dishes looked amazing, actually. The problem was me. I didn't want chicken marsala *or* Italian sausage lasagna. I wanted Blake, and from the confident way he gazed at me from across the table, he knew it.

He dug his fork into the lasagna first, blew on it, and then brought it to my lips. "Try this," he said, presenting me with the first bite as seductively as if he were offering me a chocolate-covered berry.

I opened my mouth because...well, how could I not?

He slipped the morsel of cheesy pasta goodness between my lips. Everything melted.

"Mmm," I moaned. Deliciousness.

He leaned closer to me. "Good, isn't it?"

"Heavenly."

"It's only gonna get better," he assured me. And damned if he wasn't right.

Every bite of our dinner—straight through to the rum-soaked tiramisu for dessert—was scrumptious. The red wine flowed as fast as the conversation that followed and went down just as smoothly and easily.

Surprisingly, there was no real awkwardness.

No wishing I were back at home reading my Austen/sci-fi novel instead.

And, aside from those early moments of nervousness and doubt, there was no distrust of Blake. He'd successfully and capably reeled me in and disarmed all of my well-honed defenses.

Even when we left the restaurant and shifted over to the dance club, the spell he'd cast persisted. The Crypt was so named because it was in the basement of the building, and we had to descend a lengthy flight of stairs to get inside. On the way down, Blake once again reassured me that we could leave anytime.

"So don't worry, Vicky. I'm not gonna jump you. No one's even gonna force you to dance, if you don't want to." He laughed. "Just let loose and try to enjoy the music."

I took him at his word and, for the rest of the night, just let go of all expectation.

And we did dance.

He asked. I said, "Yes." He led me to the floor.

Within two minutes, he'd left me utterly breathless, and not just from the physical exertion.

We only had one drink each at the club, and our wine from dinner was wearing off, so it wasn't the alcohol either.

It was *freedom*.

Freedom from judgment—my own.

Somewhere in the middle of that sparkling dance floor,

with Nineties-era club music intermixed with current hits, all playing loud and insistently, I recognized just how much self-recrimination was a part of my daily routine. How often I'd chastise myself for the relationship mistakes of my past. And I didn't need that tonight.

So, I followed Blake's directive. I let loose. I enjoyed the music. And I danced, face-to-face with him, arms swinging and, occasionally, clinging. But, mostly, we were just free...together. At one with the ever-changing melodies and the flashes of colored light.

True to his word, he didn't jump me. And when the clock struck midnight and this little Cinderella wanted to go home, he didn't persuade me to stay a moment longer. He just said, "No problem. Let's get you back to Mirabelle Harbor."

Which was why, when he told me he was going to walk me up to my apartment, I didn't think twice or try to parry the idea. I'd forgotten that "later" was, in fact, "now."

"It's 12:30, Blake," I said when we reached my doorway. "I need to get to bed."

He nodded. "I know. I'm still planning to kiss you goodnight, though. Unless you tell me otherwise."

I couldn't bring myself to resist that.

But I procrastinated just a little. "It'll probably be a quick kiss, though, right? I mean, you have to get home to Winston."

"Nope. Derek and Olivia are dog sitting him tonight. I told them I had plans. Late evening plans."

"Oh," I murmured and then just stood there staring at him.

Still, he waited patiently until I actually rolled my eyes and said the words aloud. "Fine, Blake. I'm not saying no to a kiss from you, okay?"

At that, he grinned and motioned toward the door. "Do you want your neighbors to watch us—however briefly? If not, maybe we should step inside." He shrugged. "Your choice."

It was a sneaky tactic, but an effective one. Blake knew I didn't have exhibitionist tendencies.

I unlocked my door and ushered him into my apartment. Then I closed the door. Firmly.

"We're talking just a kiss, right?" A totally lame clarification, but I wanted to be clear.

"Unless you tell me otherwise," he said again. Then he licked his lips.

A wolf. That was who he was. And I was no longer Cinderella. I was Little Red Riding Hood, lost in the forest and in big trouble.

Napoleon was nowhere in sight, but I trusted that my cat was fine. One glance at his bowl told me he'd eaten a good dinner. And the apartment looked exactly as we'd left it. No break-ins. No appliance malfunctions. Basically, there was no excuse I could use to distract Blake from his mission. And, honestly, I didn't really want to try.

He waited only until he knew he had my full attention, but he didn't just swoop in—mouth to mouth.

No. He was too good at seduction for that.

He placed the tip of his thumb at my temple and traced the side of my face with agonizing slowness. He didn't stop until he could cup my chin and draw me closer to him. But, still, he didn't kiss my lips. He dipped his head to my neck and worked his way upward until I was straining for his touch—my head against the door, the rest of me completely open to him.

By the time our lips finally met, I couldn't take the anticipation for a second longer. I wanted the heat of his mouth to warm mine. I wanted to taste him and to lose all thought in the warring chaos of sensation.

Blake wasn't in complete control anymore, but it wasn't as if I held much control either. There was no mental filter between my desires and my actions. None of the usual arguments telling me to behave myself or warning me of all the things that could go wrong. An absence of the tickertape of red flags that I typically kept tabs on so my heart wouldn't get crushed again.

These lack of worries brought with them a delicious freedom.

He stripped off my jeans. I didn't stop him because I was too busy unbuttoning his blue shirt and pushing away the fabric so I'd have clear access to his torso.

I kissed his chest, put my mouth around one hard male nipple, then the other.

Blake groaned and responded by yanking down my panties, tensing his hands around my hips, and squeezing until the space between his palms and my flesh was nonexistent. Then, keeping the connection between us airtight, he slid one of his hands toward my belly, the tips of his fingers brushing against my clit, pressing and sliding and teasing until I fully opened that part of myself to him, too. He thrust two of his fingers deep within me, kissing me fiercely at the same time, so when I cried out his name, the sound was muffled.

He pulled back and grinned, unable to disguise his look of pride.

"Now, aren't you glad we weren't standing out in your hallway, huh?" he whispered in my ear with a wicked little chuckle.

I chuckled, too. I should have felt embarrassed...or anxious...or some other unfortunate though familiar emotion. But I didn't. I felt only the pleasure of his touch. Undiluted excitement. The divine weightlessness of my limbs.

Perhaps the embarrassment and the anxiety would flood my body later, but I was conscious of the fact that it hadn't happened yet. I felt the strangest sense of clarity.

I wanted him.

I wanted Blake Michaelsen.

Completely and utterly and without any strings or

expectations.

And this was okay because it was exactly what he wanted. We were two consenting adults. If we both chose to have a fling, who could stop us, right?

I wasn't sure how, precisely, I expressed my invitation to him to stay the night, but I was fully cognizant of what I was doing.

For his part, Blake was wholeheartedly willing but undeniably surprised.

"You sure, Vicky?"

"What? You need your propositions to be engraved in gold leaf or something?" I said with a laugh.

He shook his head. "I'm just a little stunned that you didn't make me work harder to get the green light. I was prepared to launch a full initiative. I'd barely gotten started here."

I raised an eyebrow. "Ah. I see. Your one- or two-night stands are only truly successful if you win them by skill of seduction, eh? It doesn't count if, say, a woman simply makes a decision that she wants you for the night...with none of the game-playing bullshit."

He stared at me, mute.

I reached into his back pocket and withdrew his wallet. I pressed the leather against his chest. "There's got to be a condom somewhere in there, right?"

He nodded.

"Good. Find it." Then I pulled off my shirt, unhooked my bra, and threw them both on the floor. "I'm getting into bed. You coming?"

Blake's jaw dropped and there was a long moment of complete silence. I kept to my course of action and just wandered—totally naked—into my bedroom and without looking back. I was, oddly, at peace with my sudden and unanticipated decision, and I would remain so whether Blake followed me in here or not. Though I desperately hoped for the former.

The problems I'd had with relationships in the past had been all because of over-expectation. That wasn't the case this time.

Not. At. All.

Blake had already and insistently admitted that he didn't do the love thing. That his feelings were all in the lust department. And that his attentions to me weren't romantic but strategic. He just wanted to sleep with me...to get laid and, then, to let me go. I had no reason not to trust this truth.

So, since he only cared about my body and not my heart, mind, or soul, I didn't have to worry about losing anything significant—except, maybe, ending my long stretch of sexual frustration. And that was no great sacrifice.

He slipped into the room. He'd gotten rid of his shoes, socks, jeans, and he was wearing just a pair of thin black boxers and waving the condom packet like it was a flag of surrender.

"I'm entirely at your mercy," he whispered, setting the packet down with great deliberateness on my nightstand and ditching the boxers before crawling into bed next to me.

"I'll be gentle," I said.

"Not too gentle, I hope." He grinned. "I want you so much."

"I want you, too." I didn't wait for him to officially hand over the reins of leadership, I just took them. I pushed him to the mattress, covered his bare body with mine, and brought my lips to his.

After that, everything just flowed from one moment to the next, like some wild river. Lost in his touch, time for me turned fluid.

But aside from murmuring his name and hearing him murmur mine, Blake and I didn't speak again for the longest time. Given how talkative he usually was, this should have surprised me. It didn't, though. We were still communicating—just nonverbally—and that conversation was rich in subtext.

The way he looked at me, pressed his lips against mine, moved deep inside me. It was question and response. Call and reply. Repeated and, yet, always new.

I hadn't expected that more than our bodies would connect. But we were fully *together* in these moments. He touched *me,* not just my skin, with a tenderness that stole my breath. A raw reality that I knew would haunt me.

Maybe this was a typical kind of hookup for him, but it wasn't for me. It wasn't remotely like anything I'd experienced before with other men. This thing with Blake might be short-lived, but I already knew it wouldn't be easy to forget.

Conversation, using actual words, returned sometime later.

I stretched in bed next to him, my limbs aching in a blissful way, a sheen of sweat on my chest, and a level of exhaustion that was hard to ignore. The red glow of the digital clock said it was 1:43 a.m., a couple of hours past my normal bedtime.

Blake's eyes were drooping, but there was a smile on his lips, which widened when he realized I was staring at him.

"Hey, beautiful," he said. "How are you feeling?"

"Deliciously tired."

"I like the sound of that." He slung an arm around my waist, splaying his palm across the small of my back and drawing me to him like a slow-moving magnet. He devoured my mouth for several seconds. "Yep. Definitely delicious."

"And exhausted," I repeated. "You wore me out."

"Excellent. We can take a nap until you've recharged and, then, go for round two."

"You're insatiable."

"You won't hear me denying it, Vicky. Not with you."

The hand on my back slid further down until he reached my bottom and started caressing me. I could feel the heat flaring up between us again, and I gasped for air.

"Not sure I can take my hands off you," he said. "I might find myself getting into trouble at the high school just so I can score a detention with you."

I laughed. "I don't usually get assigned detention duty. You might end up alone in an empty classroom with Janice Keen, the lunchroom lady."

He made a comical face. "She's still there? She's gotta be, like, eighty-something now. That woman's been scaring high-school students since I was a freshman."

"Hey, I like Mrs. Keen."

"You would."

I ran my fingers through his dark hair and nibbled sleepily on his earlobe. "Mmm. Well, it's not like she's really going to see us together. Nor will anyone else, for that matter. As it is, I'm probably going to have to avoid your sister at least until Christmas, or she might figure it out."

His hand stilled and his eyes opened wider. "You, uh, aren't going to tell Shar we were...together?"

"Are you insane? *Of course not.* That would be foolish, especially for just a night of lust and self-delusion." I grinned at Blake. "I mean, c'mon. You know how she is. Within a half hour, she'll have us married and living in a house on Cherry Street with three kids. Not wise. So I hope you don't plan to tell her either."

"But you're not ashamed of this, are you?" He motioned between us with his fingers. "Regretting it?"

"No. But I don't want to be known around Mirabelle Harbor as one of your conquests, either."

He pulled away from me and sat up. "You make it sound like I'm not only a manwhore, but a damned untrustworthy one." He looked hurt and, then, infuriated.

Like I'd insulted him just because I'd remembered his "I don't believe in love" argument with too much accuracy.

"Blake, listen to me. I was paying attention to what you've been saying—in my classroom, at the park, in your apartment. You *told* me you were only interested in a fling. A one- or two-night stand. And I accepted this—" I motioned between us, mimicking his actions, "based on *your* terms, not mine. Your sister is one of my dearest friends, and when there was tension between you and me, she picked up on it right away and worried about us. And that was just for the Homecoming thing. If she knew about this, too, she'd freak out. I'm sure you don't want that."

But Blake didn't answer. He clenched his jaw, crossed his arms, and stared into the darkness of the room with an even darker expression on his face.

"I don't understand how you can be mad about this," I whispered. "It's what you said you wanted."

He shook his head.

Okay, maybe I should have let it drop because, clearly, he was upset and we were both tired, but I was frustrated now and genuinely puzzled. "Explain this to me, Blake. How am I wrong here? How have I hurt *you?*"

When he still refused to answer, I got pissed. "Seriously? Our relationship—such that it is—has been nothing but a big game to you since the beginning. Since our first meeting at the school. *All* of your flirting, your innuendos, your propositions—now you're, what? Angry because I *chose* to have sex with you tonight with no strings attached rather than having sex with you because I got *tricked* into it by thinking you really cared about me? You'd prefer that I'd been fooled and seduced? Is that it?"

"No!" he shouted finally. But I wasn't sure I believed him.

"Then what's this *really* about?" I asked.

"I can't—" he began. "It's just—just that you think so poorly of me, Vicky. I'm not ready for marriage or anything, okay? I never hid that. But it kills me that I'm nothing more than a dirty little secret to you."

I stared at him, mouth agape. "I never said that."

"You implied it." He jumped out of bed, grabbed his boxers, and bolted out of the room.

Napoleon meowed loudly from somewhere near the kitchen. Blake, wrestling with clothes and keys, banged into something—accidentally or deliberately, I couldn't be sure—and my cat screeched in response.

"Goodbye," Blake called out before the front door slammed. Whether that was intended for me or my cat was just as unclear but, by the time I managed to find a long t-shirt to put on and get to the door, he was gone.

What the hell had just happened here?

~*Blake*~

Max's Pub stayed open until three a.m. on Saturday nights. Thank God.

And Gina was bartending, which helped. She'd poured me a few fingers of my favorite vodka before I even sat down.

"You look like crap," she observed, pushing the drink toward me from across the bar. "What happened?"

I had no fucking idea.

"I have no fucking idea, Gina, but I don't want to talk about it," I growled, swallowing about half the vodka in one gulp. It burned its way down my throat.

She shrugged. "Whatever you say." Then she went back to stacking glasses behind the counter.

"There's this woman—" I began.

"With you, there's always a woman," Gina shot back.

"Yeah, well, not one like *her*. She's...different."

"Really? Someone I know?"

I shook my head. Maybe Gina knew her, maybe she didn't. Either way, I wasn't gonna tell.

"You don't know her name?"

"Of course I know her name," I said, gulping some more vodka.

"Ah." Gina paused, crossed her arms, and smiled at me. "You aren't going to kiss and tell with this lady, huh? Wow. She *must* be different."

"We slept together tonight," I blurted. I hadn't had nearly enough to drink—not yet—so I knew it wasn't the alcohol talking. Guess I just wanted someone to listen to me.

"It didn't go well? Performance issues?"

"*WHAT?* Jeez, Gina. No. Everything in that sense was fine. Great, actually."

"I'm not understanding the problem then, Blake. That's usually a good thing, in your opinion, right?"

"Usually, yes."

"So...why the sad eyes, the need to numb yourself with alcohol, the uncharacteristically glum reaction to getting laid?"

I finished my first vodka and pointed at the glass. Didn't say another word until she'd poured me another drink. "She doesn't trust me enough to want more," I whispered.

"When did you start wanting more than that?" She looked genuinely perplexed. "Not that it's a bad thing...just, you know, really surprising."

"I *don't* want more! I've never wanted more. So, shit. I don't know. I'm just angry."

"You're angry that she doesn't want something that you...um, *also* don't want?" She rubbed her temples. "Maybe it's just because it's after two a.m., but I'm still really confused and I don't understand the issue."

"Neither did she."

Gina came to stand right in front of me, leaning over the counter until we were nearly at eye level. "Did it ever occur to you that things may have changed for you, Blake?

That you do, actually, want more than a quickie with *her*...this mysterious woman whose name you're being too honorable for the first time *ever* to tell me?"

"I'd be stupid to want that."

"Maybe. But let me ask you this—what would you have wanted to be different? What did you expect from her tonight that you didn't get?"

It was a fair question. One I had to struggle to put into words, and when they came out, they still sounded lame. "That she would've cared about more than just our physical connection. That she would've felt more respect for me. That she'd want to introduce me to her friends or not be ashamed to be seen with me in public."

Oh, shit. I sounded like a whiny teenage girl. And Gina was looking at me as if I'd just sprouted alien antennas and turned a revolting shade of green.

"Never mind," I said as I finished my second drink in one long swallow. "Just pour me another vodka."

"Are you sure that's a good idea—"

"Hell, Gina. I fucking *know* it's not a good idea, okay?"

She winced, but she pushed the vodka bottle toward me and let me choose.

"Sorry," I said, motioning the bottle away and waiting for her to remove it. "You're right. I should stop for tonight. Please just ignore me. I know I'm being an ass."

"Look, Blake," she said in a very gentle voice. "Maybe I'm going out on a limb here, but it sounds like you really care about this woman. And you're hurt and maybe worried that she might not care about you to the same degree. Does that ring true?"

I covered my eyes with my palms to keep from glaring at her. Damn, but it just killed me to have to admit something like that. Problem was, that was the only explanation that made any bloody sense.

Finally, I looked up at her and nodded slightly. Gina nodded back. Then she leaned over and pecked my cheek and left me alone to stew in my thoughts.

When closing time came, I paid my tab, tipped Gina extra big, and left the bar without a word.

Maybe it was because not even Winston was waiting at home for me (he was still with my brother and his wife until morning) that the loneliness hit me harder than usual. It was 3:14 a.m., only an hour and a half since I'd stormed out of Vicky's place, but it felt like eons.

I missed her already.

I should've stayed and fought with her in person, rather than just arguing with her in my head. I needed to tell her how I was feeling—wasn't that what normal people did? Expressed themselves when something in a relationship was bothering them?

Our relationship—such that it is... Those were her words. She didn't quite see us as having a real relationship, but that felt wrong to me. And *now* felt like the time I absolutely had to tell her this.

I knew, even as I was punching her number into my cell phone, that this plan of action was probably not my best idea ever, but I couldn't fight the compulsion. And, to be honest, just hearing her voice on the other end was justification enough for me. Didn't give a damn how much I'd likely regret it later.

"Blake?" she said, sleepy but still so proper and polite.

"I n-need to talk t-to you," I said or, rather, stuttered, which was a first for me.

In any case, she had no trouble understanding me because she replied, "It's after three in the morning."

"I don't care. I can come over now."

"I *do* care," she said. "Have you been drinking? Because, if you have, you shouldn't be driving anywhere in any case."

She was right. I'd kinda forgotten about that since, as usual, I'd just walked to Max's and back. Plus, I'd stopped after only two drinks and wasn't even close to feeling buzzed. But I didn't want to let this subject drop, and I didn't want to have this conversation on the phone. "Well, *you* can come over to my place then."

She sighed. "No, Blake, I can't. It's really late, and I'd hit the point of exhaustion hours ago. I'm way beyond that now. So, please, just go to bed and let me do the same. We can talk tomorrow—or, really, later today—okay? We'll both be able to think more clearly then."

It wasn't okay. I'd never be able to fall asleep. And I didn't like the implication that I wasn't thinking clearly now. I was seeing everything clearer than I ever had. I told her this. "Vicky, c'mon. Just drive to my apartment and we'll—"

"I already said no, Blake, and I meant it. The answer is no. *N.O.* Do you hear me? It's still no. Not tonight. And if you somehow manage to come over here, I'll tell you upfront that I won't let you in. Not even if you pound on the door or yell in the hallway or cause a scene. Our date night is over and so is this conversation. Understand me?"

"I understand, but—"

"Glad to hear it," she said, a note of finality ringing loud and clear in her voice. "Goodnight, Blake."

"Vicky—"

But there was a click and I knew she'd hung up. Shit, shit, shit.

CHAPTER ELEVEN

~Blake~

I couldn't say when or how I finally fell asleep, I just knew when I woke up that there was a cloud of dread hanging over me like some character in a cartoon. Like I was the only one in the picture being rained on. And I found myself weirdly dispirited, hoping Armageddon might come early so I wouldn't have to deal with the consequences of the day.

Note to self: Late-night dialing (even when it was not technically drunk dialing) was *never* a good idea. Why hadn't I remembered this from when I was in school?

Two vodkas and a long chat with the bartender did not a hangover make. But I was as embarrassed this morning as if I'd had a wild bender of a night. Embarrassed that I'd effed up my date with Vicky by bolting out of her bedroom, by calling her at three a.m. and, worst of all, by getting so damned attached to her in the first place.

I replayed in my head every single conversation we'd ever had against her comments to me last night. And, hell. They didn't make me look good.

Maybe I'd teased and taunted her a little too much this past month. She probably didn't see it as the flirtatious foreplay I'd intended. And maybe I'd come across as a prick by insisting that love was some kind of foolish illusion. But it was. Or, at least, I'd always thought it was...until recently. I'd only been trying to speak honestly about that.

Pretty much the only thing I knew for sure was that I owed her an apology for bolting out of her apartment and then pestering her after I left. I was mad and I was hurt, but I knew better than to do that. What did it say about my screwed up feelings for this woman that I was suddenly breaking my own well-established rules?

And this crazy attraction to her was supposed to *end* after we'd slept together. But it had only gotten stronger. Why? Could Gina have nailed it? Had I actually changed?

My shift at the radio station started at noon today, and it was already after ten right now. I didn't want to wait for hours to speak with Vicky, so I took a shower, threw on some clean clothes, and drove over to her place before I lost my nerve.

My heart was hammering in my chest like I'd just run a four-minute mile when I rang the outside buzzer.

"Yes?" she said, her voice sounding wary, tired.

I swallowed and tried to push the words out, but I couldn't speak. Just hearing her again brought back a rush of memories. Of holding her, kissing her, listening to her whispers and moans.

"Is there someone out there?" she said, with more force this time.

I finally cleared my throat and managed to reply. "It's me, Vicky. Um, Blake."

There was a long pause. Too long. I knew she was debating her options.

I squeezed my eyes shut and tried to prepare myself for the possibility that she wouldn't let me in. I was ready to

145

explain that I could only stay for a short while. That I wouldn't bother her for long. That I was just here to apologize in person. But I was having a devil of a time getting my mouth to cooperate.

Finally, I heard the buzzing sound that allowed me to enter the lobby, so I let myself inside before she could change her mind.

She was waiting for me when I got to her apartment, peeking into the hallway like a little kid who'd been reluctantly sent to answer the door.

I bowed my head and whispered through the crack, "Thanks for letting me come up. I just came over to talk to you in person, but I'll be out of your hair in ten minutes, okay?"

She pulled the door open all the way and let me in. "Okay."

I studied her face when I was inside and could see that she didn't just sound tired, she looked it, too. Guilt twisted in my gut over having caused that as well.

"Look, Vicky—I'm sorry. I shouldn't have snapped at you last night. I shouldn't have stormed out. And I really shouldn't have called you so late. Up until all that happened, it had been an amazing night. I can't tell you how sorry I am that I ruined it."

She tilted her head and sent me a soft, sad smile, sighing like I'd drained all the breath out of her. "Don't worry about it," she said.

"But I *am* going to worry about it because I don't want to make that mistake with you next time."

She shook her head. "There isn't going to be a next time. This was a one-night stand, remember? Easy come, easy go." She shrugged like she totally didn't care. "So, really, it's fine."

"It's *not* fine," I ground out. "Because I'd like to go out with you again."

"Well, life isn't always about what *you'd* like, is it,

Blake?" She crossed her arms and I felt a sizzle of anger radiating from her body. She was tamping it down. Trying to control it.

Fury wasn't exactly a good thing, but it sure as hell beat indifference. I was oddly encouraged.

"I get how you could be mad," I told her. "I wasn't at my best last night. Calling you so late after going to Max's was really stupid, but I was trying to process everything, and you were the only one I wanted to talk to."

"You didn't want to talk to me when you were here, though," she countered. "Or even when you called. You just wanted to argue."

That may have been true, but I wasn't thrilled to hear it and, besides, it wasn't as though she'd been completely without fault. She'd been pretty damn insulting to me last night. I reminded her of this.

"Really?" She raised her eyebrows. "*More* insulting than you've been to me *all* month? I don't think so, Blake." She turned her back to me and began riffling through a stack of papers on her kitchen counter a few feet away. "Hardly hero material," she murmured in a low tone, but not so low that I couldn't hear it.

I felt my temper crackle and break. "Forgive me for not being perfect, Vicky. I'm not a fucking fictional character or some literary fantasy man of yours. I'm a *real* guy with real flaws. I'm not proud of them, but I'm working on being better. I'm not going to be able to read your mind, though, or fulfill every romantic scenario you've ever dreamed up so, sometimes, we have to live in the actual world."

She took a step back and stared at me hard. "I'm well aware that book boyfriends aren't real, Blake, but heroes are. They're the kind of men that others can rely on. The kind that are there for the long haul. Not the kind who'll say anything to get a woman into bed and then become all insecure and possessive when she doesn't consider him trustworthy. You say you can't read my mind? Okay, I'll tell you what I'm thinking. That you're just in that 'lusting, obsessive, delusional, needy' phase right now, and that you got angry last night because, for once, you weren't the one calling the shots. You wanted a fling? Well, *voilà,* you got one. That decision was on me and I'm not going to regret it—but I'm not going to repeat it either. If nothing else, your behavior since we slept together has convinced me that I was right to hold out only for love. Maybe I'll never find it, but these kind of casual hookups and this game-playing crap of yours isn't close enough to the real thing for me. So, just—just let it go. Find someone else's head to screw with."

I opened my mouth to speak but no words came out. She thought I was playing mind games? Did she not hear a freakin' thing I'd been trying to say to her?

Apparently not.

But my tongue and lips weren't working in tandem with my brain. I was feeling a bunch of emotions but utterly incapable of expressing any of them. So, when she glanced between me and the door, I just stalked away from her again. The second time in less than twelve hours, which was a record for me. But what else could I do?

I was angry to the point of vibrating by the time I got to Derek and Olivia's house to pick up Winston, but I knew for damned sure that I didn't want to talk about Vicky with my brother or his wife.

"What's wrong with you?" Derek asked. "Did someone cut you off on the drive over here?"

No. Someone cut me off in every other way, though.

"I'm fine," I assured my brother.

"You don't look fine. Need an ear to listen? Someone to bounce ideas off of today? Just tell me how I can help."

"Thanks," I said, as Winston came hobbling toward me, "but no one can help. It's a lost cause."

"Nothing's a lost cause, Blake. C'mon. We can talk it

out."

I shook my head. "Not this."

"If you change your mind—" Derek began.

"You'll be the first to know." I pointed at my dog. "Thank you for watching Winston last night. Sorry to grab and run, but I gotta go. My shift starts in twenty minutes."

Before Derek could try to man-hug me or anything, I got out of his house. I returned my furry best friend to the safe familiarity of my apartment, made sure he had enough food and water, and then walked across the street to the radio station.

Vicky's words dogged my every step, though. She was flat-out wrong about nearly all of it but, once again, I was struggling to articulate why and how.

This picture she painted of me as a major asshat was what bothered me the most. I'd been labeled a lot of negative things in my life. I'd been called impulsive, immature, cocky, and reckless for as long as I could remember. Women typically thought of me as a bad boy—a sexy one, if I was lucky. But no one had ever accused me of being *unheroic*. That was an unhappy first.

As Amelia and I switched places in the 102.5 booth, she shot me a worried glance. "Everything okay with your dog?" she asked.

"Winston? Yeah, he's still recovering from the accident, but he's making good progress."

"Your family then? No illnesses or anything?"

"They're fine, too. Everybody's healthy."

"Then what on Earth is wrong with you today? You look like someone died."

I scowled at her. Amelia was sweet, but she was too damn curious.

"Your shift is over, isn't it?" I tapped the face of my wristwatch. "Go home. I'm sure you have some friends or relatives or next-door neighbors who'd welcome one of your well-meaning inquisitions, but I've got a four-hour show to do now."

"You having trouble sleeping? Eating? Getting it up?"

My jaw dropped open. What the hell was with all of these people questioning my sexual performance? "None of the above. Now leave."

"So, it's probably about a woman then, right?"

"Jeez, Amelia! Stop. Your. Prying."

She leaned against the doorframe and just stared at my head while I pretended to organize the few items in front of me. I fiddled with the mic, but before I could click it on, Amelia rushed over and squeezed my shoulders. She planted a wet kiss on my cheek and whispered, "Whatever happened, and whomever it happened with, it'll be all right, Blake. Love can be hard sometimes. Just hang in there."

To my absolute horror, I started to get misty-eyed right in the middle of the booth. I ducked my head so Amelia wouldn't see, muttered a quick "Yeah, thanks," and launched into the show a full three minutes early.

"It's nearly noon at 102.5 LOVE FM. Blake Michaelsen stepping in here as we get ready for a relaxing Sunday afternoon. We've got a great lineup of romantic songs headed your way, and a few fun announcements. Stay tuned for more! And to start us off, how about a pair of classic tunes by Elton John?"

As "I Guess That's Why They Call It the Blues" started to play, my coworker finally slipped out of the booth, blowing me a kiss before she left.

I managed a grateful wave, but I was so damned relieved Amelia was gone. How could she read me so well? My emotions were insanely out of whack today and, clearly, it showed. It would be better to limit the number of witnesses.

My brain literally ached from thinking so hard and from trying to control every feeling. Homecoming Week kicked off with the car wash in an hour, and I'd promised the students on the committee that I'd give them an on-the-air shout out. Much as I was still pissed at Vicky and hurt by her god-awful low opinion of me, it wasn't like I'd go back on my word to the kids.

But as the first Elton John hit shifted into the second— "Sad Songs"—I couldn't help but wonder if I'd make it through the next hour, let alone the next four. The lyrics were starting to get to me. Not in the usual they're-trite-and-annoying sort of way, but in the they-kinda-make-sense way. And that worried the crap out of me.

I scanned the playlist.

"Open Arms" by Journey was coming up.

"Hurts So Good" by John Cougar Mellencamp followed.

And then there were about a dozen other songs that, in some way, reminded me of the Mademoiselle. I mean, she was *everywhere* in my mind. I thought of her whenever a popular Eighties tune played, since most of them were on my Homecoming dance playlist. I thought of her whenever there was a song about pain caused by a romantic relationship. Or whenever there was the slightest mention of honesty and openness with a lover. And, of course, whenever there was a lyric that referenced France or so much as used a French phrase. ELO's "Hold on Tight to Your Dream" (*Accroches-Toi À Ton Rêve*) had me gritting my teeth and needing to escape the booth for a mug of extra-strong coffee.

Unfortunately, this turned out to be a lousy idea.

Both of my bosses—Doug and Leonard—were sitting in the break room going over paperwork when I walked in.

"Blake," they said in unison.

"Hey, just getting some coffee. I'll be back in the booth in a sec." I grabbed a mug and started pouring.

"You've got your next few songs already scheduled, right?" Doug asked.

"Of course."

"Good!" he said. "Sit down with us for a few minutes."

Leonard waved a sheet of paper in the air. "Your buddy Trevor Cayne from the *Gazette* sent over a copy of the piece he ran in yesterday's issue about the high school's Homecoming."

"We loved that new slogan you came up with for the station," Doug added.

"'The Heartbeat of Mirabelle Harbor!'" Leonard enthused. "That's inspired."

I gulped about a third of my coffee, wishing it were spiked with rum or schnapps or...anything. "Glad you liked it," I told them, taking a few steps toward the door.

"No, don't leave yet," Doug said. "We've got some really exciting ideas for upcoming promotions and we'd like you—"

"Yeah, whatever," I interrupted, so rudely that my parents would've slapped my face if they were still alive. But if I didn't get away from my bosses and their inane grins, I'd probably knock out one of them. That wouldn't bode well for my job security.

"He's not a morning person," I heard Leonard say to Doug as I slipped out of the room.

"Yeah, but it's almost one in the afternoon..." Doug countered.

I didn't stick around to hear the rest. It was all I could do to try to finish my shift without getting myself fired.

A few hours later, though, just as J.J. took over the reins, both of my bosses motioned me out of the booth and into the hall.

"Guys, look, I'm sorry," I said. "I'm having a really rotten day. I just need to get home—"

Doug put his hand on my arm to silence me. "It's okay. We talked to Amelia. We know you're dealing with an *affaire du coeur*."

Fuck.

"I'm fine," I insisted.

Leonard nodded knowingly. "We've all been there,

Blake. Like Bryan Adams said, 'It's Only Love.'"

Somebody needed to pull the trigger and put an end to my suffering. Now, if possible. "Um, thanks," I said, leaning away from Doug's kindly grasp.

"There's nothing like music to bring out the full depth of your pain," Leonard added. "Like the way salt draws out water from a sliced tomato."

I stared at him. "Okay."

"Just be aware that you're not alone, Blake," said Doug. "Others have been in that same pit of despair. Musicians *know* what you're feeling. They composed songs about it. Wrote lyrics that expressed the heartache. Listen to their wisdom, and let yourself feel the beautiful sadness."

"Not really helping," I murmured.

Leonard nodded. "When all else fails, order your favorite carryout, light a few candles, and put on some Barry Connelly. Allow yourself to wallow in the misery. You can only start to come up after you've hit rock bottom."

I managed a respectful nod. "Wise words," I said before finally escaping the two of them and literally running back to my apartment.

"Holy hell," I said to Winston. "You have no idea how much I missed you." I picked him up and stroked his fur, being careful not to press too hard near his head bruises or his bandaged front leg. He was healing, for which I was incredibly grateful, but I just realized I couldn't even look at my own dog without thinking of Vicky. Damn her.

"What d'ya say we order up an early dinner and watch some Sunday night football?"

Winston barked and wagged his tail.

But when the delivery guy from Sloppy Joe's arrived with my burger and fries, all I could think about was Vicky and the burgers we'd eaten together after that long day at the vet.

Watching anything on TV made me think of her, too.

And the radio was the worst of all. I refused to even tune in to 102.5, but every other station seemed to have conspired to play love songs from Tom Odell's "Can't Pretend" to Lifehouse's "Everything."

I couldn't even play the music on my own iPod because I'd shared so many of my favorite songs with her that they mingled with my memories. I was screwed.

After about three hours, I gave in and streamed a few Barry Connelly tunes on my laptop. Didn't know what caused me more agony, having to listen to all of those "ooooh, babys" in his big hit "You're the One," or having to admit to myself that his sappy, overly simplistic, utterly repetitive lyrics suddenly resonated with me on a deep level.

If this wasn't a sign that Armageddon might be coming after all, I didn't know what was.

~Vicky~

Stephanie Little bounced up to me on Monday afternoon, bursting with excitement. "Matt tallied up the sales from the car wash yesterday, and we made *twice* the profit that we made last year!" she gushed. "Blake is *amazing*. We wouldn't have gotten nearly as many customers without his radio announcements. Did you hear him, Mademoiselle?"

"Oh, yes," I said.

Whatever Blake Michaelsen's faults (and I'd been keeping a rather extensive list of them), he was a charismatic guy and had proven to be a man of his word. He'd promised the kids he'd promote their event, and he did. With gusto. I'd heard him mention the car wash at least a half-dozen times during his shift at the station, and I didn't even have my radio on for the whole four hours.

Honestly, I didn't know what my problem was, but the songs on LOVE FM were making me edgy—and a little depressed—for the first time ever. And it was so strange hearing Blake's voice when I knew him so much better now. Maybe because no matter how upbeat he tried to sound on the air, I knew he was faking it. At least a little. I'd seen him in person just two hours before and he'd looked and sounded so down, so beat. Which bothered me because I'd felt supremely justified in being mad at him...until he'd come over this morning. He seemed weirdly withdrawn and subdued, like I was the one who'd hurt *him*. It didn't make sense.

Stephanie chattered at me for a few minutes more before rushing off to one of her many after-school clubs. Glad someone, at least, had enjoyed her Sunday.

There was a foreign language department meeting scheduled to start just down the hall in Christine's room, but I didn't immediately race down to it.

Instead, I leaned against one of the cool walls of my classroom, closed my eyes, and replayed Saturday night in bed with Blake. The way he touched me until my body hummed. Until my senses were filled with him. Until I didn't think we could get any closer.

We were so fundamentally different from each other out of bed that I couldn't believe how well things worked between us beneath the covers. Still, I'd given into desire and slept with him against my better judgment.

I hadn't been lying when I told Blake that I didn't regret any of it. I couldn't bring myself to wish away *that* magical hour. But, ultimately, look at the way things had unraveled between us? It couldn't have happened faster or been more painful. Some people just weren't meant to be together.

The other foreign language teachers were already in the room when I nearly skidded into the meeting, a full two minutes late.

Christine raised her eyebrows when she saw me. "You okay, Vicky? Is something going on?"

Lisa, Marcie, and Janet all turned to look at me with concern.

"Nothing to worry about," I said, but apparently not convincingly enough because Janet crossed her arms and shook her head in disbelief.

"We're your friends. We worry," she said.

"Parle-nous," Marcie said in her impeccable French. *Talk to us.*

"Yeah," added Lisa. "Spill."

I cleared my throat. "I don't want to derail our meeting—"

"We can discuss the Foreign Language Fête later," Lisa interrupted.

Christine, our department head, was quick to agree. "Seriously, Vicky, we've got four weeks to plan the event. It can wait. What's got you looking so flustered?"

I closed the classroom door and sank into one of the chairs, never appreciating my teaching colleagues more than I did at this moment. Maybe my love life sucked the big one, but how lucky I was to have friends like these. People who cared about me, even when I was an emotional wreck and could barely concentrate long enough to compose a complete sentence. It was a wonder that I'd made it through a full school day. But how was I going to make it through the rest of the week? The Homecoming dance?

I took a deep breath. "So, remember how we all saw Blake Michaelsen fighting that night a few weeks ago?"

"When we left The Lounge," Lisa said. "At the beginning of September, right?"

I nodded. "Well, that same week, the kids on the Homecoming committee voted to have him be the DJ for the dance this Friday. And he accepted."

My friends looked at me expectantly. "And...so?" Janet asked.

"And so we've spent a lot of time together lately," I

managed. "And things are kind of awkward between us now." I told them briefly about him coming to the meetings here in the high school, running into him at the park a couple of times, that day at the animal hospital with Winston, and a very PG-version of our Saturday night date.

Marcie tilted her blond head and squinted at me. "Why do I get the feeling that you've left out the most interesting bits?"

I fought a blush, but I only shook my head. Blake might have loose lips when it came to dating—I actually had no idea what kinds of things he told his buddies about the women he'd gotten involved with—but I'd never been a kiss-n-tell type.

When my friends realized I wasn't going to give them a play by play of Saturday night, they turned their attention toward something more productive: Psychoanalyzing Blake Michaelsen.

Christine asked a few questions about Winston and offered a partial theory about Blake's behavior. "It might be hard for him to put himself out there emotionally, even though he doesn't seem to have a problem speaking with women," she said. "But being conversational isn't the same thing as being *open*. It might be easier for someone very guarded to be more authentic with a pet."

"Yeah," Lisa said. "Maybe because you saw him at a particularly vulnerable time, he thinks you might be able to tell the difference between the real Blake that only those closest to him know and the DJ persona that he shows most of the rest of the world."

This rang uncomfortably true. If he'd felt his real self were being judged by me, he'd be more hurt than if he just thought I was taking shots at his social veneer. Especially since he was so careful to control that social perception. Had I made the mistake of treating both sides of him interchangeably?

"That makes sense," I agreed. "But how healthy is it to

be around someone with such a split personality? That can't be a good thing."

Christine shrugged. "No one is one-hundred percent consistent. You're not. None of us are." She motioned with her hand to include everyone in the room. "But if you give the guy a chance, he just might surprise you."

Her words echoed Julia's advice that night at Drew's Diner for the Quest group gathering. Sometimes first impressions were wrong.

"It's important to go into any relationship with open eyes," Janet advised. "You're totally justified in being cautious, but that's different from being judgmental. Unless you have reason to believe he means you harm, maybe it's worth giving him a chance, eh?"

"And he's pretty hot," Marcie interjected. "You've certainly chosen worse boyfriends before."

Everyone burst out laughing, me loudest of all. My friends had seen me through the emotional roller coaster of being with Philippe and with Ryan and with a handful of other guys earlier on in my teaching career. But I'd been playing it safe for so long—choosing only book boyfriends and unattainable fantasy men—that I'd forgotten that my colleagues could still remember my being "in love" with real people. That they'd cheered me on when things were going well and encouraged me when the chips were down. That every single one of them had, at some point or other, tried to set me up with unattached guys they knew in the area.

I'd once asked Lisa why they'd all been trying so hard to get me to go on a date. Shouldn't they spend their energy on somebody whose relationship actually had a chance in hell of working out?

I remembered how Lisa had chuckled at that. She simply said, "Maybe, but you're the only one we know who's a true romantic. You *want* to find love, even when it feels hopeless."

No wonder they were so excited I finally had a guy in my life again, however tenuous the relationship and however challenging the man.

Their insightful comments about Blake did leave me pondering, though. His behavior definitely wasn't completely consistent, and his attitude was just as changeable.

But...I had to admit that I *had* brought considerable pre-judgment to my interactions with him and that, without my prejudice, I might have been a stronger listener and gotten to know the true Blake better.

"Just think about everything you really know to be true about him," Christine suggested. "Rather than reacting to his actions, that you may or may not know the reasons for, take time to consider what you really want to say to him. It may turn out to be a lot simpler than it seems to get to the heart of the issue."

I wasn't sure how much I believed that, but I didn't have a Plan B. So, when I finally got home that night, I sat down on my sofa—Napoleon on my lap—and thought about what I really wished I could say to Blake. What I felt was true. What I thought was fair. What I believed he deserved to know, and not just what my pride wanted me to cling to for dear life.

And then I texted him.

"Thanks for helping advertise the car wash on the air yesterday, as well as for making the *Gazette* story happen," I began. "The kids were so grateful." I paused and, before I hit SEND, I added, "And I really appreciated everything you did, too."

There. That was not only the truth, but it was good manners. If *anyone* in the community—even my worst enemy—had helped my students the way Blake had, I would have sent a thank-you note immediately. And Blake wasn't an *enemy*. Just, perhaps, a semi-frequent antagonist.

My phone buzzed.

I was pleased by the speedy response, although a little disappointed in the short reply.

Blake texted: "You're welcome."

Okay, now for the harder message to write, which also happened to be true:

"I'm sorry for the part I played in our argument this weekend. I'd been trying to be honest with you, not trying to hurt you, but I see that I did. I truly apologize for that."

I exhaled slowly and clicked SEND. For the longest time, there was no reply to this message. I'd begun to wonder if he'd gotten it at all or, conversely, if he was reacting to it by coming over to my apartment in person. When he didn't text, call, or show up on my doorstep after a full hour had gone by, I figured he was still mad and just choosing to ignore me.

But an hour after that, my phone finally buzzed again.

His response this time was marginally longer, but no more revealing of his emotions. He wrote:

"I'm sorry, too, Vicky. See you at the dance on Friday."

And that was it. Far worse than anger, this had the cold ring of indifference.

CHAPTER TWELVE

~*Blake*~

Wednesday afternoon dragged like one of those days when you're ill with some unspecified virus but not quite ill enough to justify taking off work.

Not that I wasn't tempted to stay home from the radio station anyway but, aside from the usual end-of-the-month paperwork I had to finish up, I told myself that all I'd have to do was survive a couple of hours of sappy music. And I needed to get out of the apartment for a little while. I'd been moping around my place so much this week that even Winston seemed sick of me.

I sure as hell was sick of myself.

And so damned sick of thinking of Vicky. Her "apology" to me—via text, no less—still stung badly. Not that I thought she was being insincere, just that her words came across as so calm, so dispassionate. No one would doubt that Mademoiselle Bernier conducted herself as a mature adult, but she'd been playing everything far too coolly for me to know if she cared about me at all.

I needed *some* show of emotion. *Some* sign that even a

small part of her was interested in me for more than just a fling. I'd give anything to have her yell at me on the street or chew me out on the phone or even post an incoherent rant about our relationship *("such that it is...")* on Facebook or Twitter.

But, no. She was too much of a grownup for that. And, much as I respected her, I wanted her to do even one irrational, reckless act that might show her willingness to let go.

Well, she did sleep with me.

The voice in my head was insistent in reminding me of this fact. Guess that was pretty impulsive and reckless for her. What more did I want, right?

I spent almost my entire shift fantasizing about Vicky barging into the radio station and insisting that we have make-up sex in the booth during an extra-long Paul McCartney set. To feed the fantasy, I even played a half dozen of the former Beatle's big hits, starting with "Silly Love Songs." A private joke between the real me and the dream Vicky, not that the flesh-and-blood woman across town would know about it.

But I was talking long and hard with her in my mind, explaining that being with her and getting to know her over this past month had changed me. That I understood what Paul and his Wings buddies were saying. That love songs might be sentimental or touching, painful or daydream-inducing but, once a person actually experienced falling in love, the songs weren't that silly. They weren't silly at all.

When my shift finally ended, I found myself at my favorite shop in town—Between the Pages—Mirabelle Harbor's only bookstore. The owner, Jaleina Longoria, was a longtime family friend. More than that, she'd once been my brother Derek's fiancée and had still managed to stay on good terms with the family. Not an unimpressive feat.

"Blake," she said with a smile. "Long time no see. Did you finally burn through that stack of mysteries and suspense stories you picked up last time?"

"Just about," I said. "Haven't started the California legal thriller yet, but I tore through the others. Been a bit busier in the last few weeks."

Jaleina raised her eyebrows but didn't press me to explain. Not that I would have. There was probably some sort of rule about not confiding in a sibling's ex if you had no intention of confiding in the sibling.

"So, what are you looking for today? Something more historical? More action-adventure?" she asked.

"More international," I ventured. "European set, maybe. Paris. French Riviera. Something like that."

She nodded and led me to the section of the bookstore labeled "Fiction in Foreign Lands." She pointed at the shelves, her index finger tapping on the word *France*. "We've got a bunch of titles here, listed by country. But some of the books we carry with international themes are also mixed in with their literary genres. So just shout out if you don't seem to be finding what you're looking for, okay?"

"Okay. Thanks, Jaleina."

"Anytime," she said.

As she walked back to the other side of the store, I couldn't help but notice how good she looked. Gorgeous smile, beautiful breasts, legs that went on for miles. She and Derek were almost the same age, so she was a few years older than me, but I wouldn't have let that stop me from pursuing her if I were truly interested. No doubt about it, Jaleina was—and always had been—one hot lady. Too bad my tastes had turned to snooty French teachers who ignored me.

I sighed and studied the novels lined up on the shelves. Paperbacks with compelling plots that would have enticed me to buy a handful of them at almost any other time.

But I just couldn't focus on fiction.

My eyes wandered down the aisle and my body soon

followed, stopping only when I got to the set of shelves labeled "International Travel Guides." I used to spend a lot of time sifting through the books here, but I hadn't checked them out in a long while.

The ABC Travel Series took up at least half of the section:

All Around Aberdeen
Breathtaking Brittany
Captivating Copenhagen
Discovery Days in Darjeeling
Exploring Everest
And more.

But it was *Quintessential Quebec* that had me reaching for the guidebook and pulling it off the shelf.

I flipped through the table of contents. Things to do in Montreal. Visiting Quebec City. Rules of the road in French-speaking Canada. Explaining the allure of Poutine.

And somehow I found myself at the cash register, handing a few bills to Jaleina, and trying to make up a semi-logical reason for why I was buying this book instead of what I thought I'd come here for.

"Someone was recently telling me about Quebec," I said.

"Haven't been there," Jaleina replied. "I've heard it's lovely, though."

"Probably really cold for most of the year," I felt compelled to add. "But there are people who like that."

"Yeah," she said agreeably, but I could feel her very aware eyes on me, studying my facial expressions and deducing things.

"This'll make a great gift for someone who's into winter sports or Canadian travel...or other French things," I concluded.

"Did you want me to gift wrap it?"

"Uh, no. That's okay."

She handed me my change, put the book in a bag, and

lightly patted my hand, like I was a kindergartener or something. "I hope whomever you bought it for will enjoy it," she said softly.

"Thanks," I said. Then I got out of the bookstore as fast as possible, so I could spend the rest of the day hiding out in my apartment, where no one but Winston would try to read my facial expressions.

❁❃❁

The next morning, I woke up at six a.m., though not by choice.

Shar called. "You didn't forget that we're celebrating Derek and Olivia's anniversary today, did you?"

"Of course not," I mumbled into the phone. And that was mostly true. I'd remembered we were doing it today. I just hadn't remembered how early.

"Good. I'm bringing the cake and the flowers. Chance and Nia are bringing fruit salad and hot Greek coffee. You just need to pick up a dozen bagels and cream cheese and meet us at the house at five to seven, okay?"

"Okay, Shar."

"Don't. Be. Late," she warned before she finally hung up.

I groaned and Winston, who thought there might be something wrong with me, came half trotting, half limping over to the bed to check on me.

"I'm fine, little buddy," I reassured him, rubbing his soft head. "Just my demanding sister and her harebrained ideas of 'family fun' again."

My dog wagged his tail at me, and worked his way over to the door, barking encouragingly. Yes, I could get up. And, yes, I could take him out for a quick walk. He never failed to warm my heart, and his sheer presence made rising at the butt crack of dawn a little easier.

After I got dressed and got Winston outside and back in again, I rushed into the deli for the bagels and cream cheese and then over to Derek and Olivia's for their surprise breakfast.

Shar had concluded that, since the anniversary couple wouldn't be expecting their siblings to show up at seven in the morning, it would be the perfect time for all of us to help them celebrate the happy occasion.

"Because, unlike you, they *love* surprises," Shar informed me in that superior tone she enjoyed using so frequently.

And she was the one who rang the doorbell, once all of us were gathered outside of the house.

Derek opened the door in his robe. "What the hell?" he said in shock, although as soon as he saw the flowers and all the food he was grinning.

When Olivia came to stand beside him and peered out at us, we all chorused, "Happy twelfth anniversary!"

"Wow," my sister-in-law said. "What's all this?"

"We know you both have to go to work," Shar said.

"And the kids have school," Nia added. "So we don't want to disrupt your routine too much."

"But breakfast *is* the most important meal of the day," Chance contributed with a wink.

Derek and Olivia laughed.

"Get in here, you guys," my big brother said. I was the last one in the house, and Derek slapped me on the back as the others walked ahead into the kitchen. "This was very nice of you, man."

"Hey, twelve years of wedded bliss with the same woman is something worth celebrating," I said. "But I probably would have chosen to celebrate it with you a bit later in the day."

He laughed. "Same here, Bro." He pointed at the large carafe of Greek coffee Nia was holding, taking turns pouring pure caffeine into individual cups for the adults.

"Let's get us some of that."

We spread out all the food on the kitchen table, toasted Derek and Olivia with our strong coffees, and helped ourselves to breakfast in the midst of chaos. My nephews didn't need a slice of the anniversary cake Shar brought to give them a satanic sugar high—their spirits were already buoyant. But as I glanced around the room, I realized a lot of joy lived here.

"You're quiet this morning," my sister said around bites of a cream-cheese-slathered blueberry bagel.

"I'm still half asleep," I admitted. "Although this coffee Nia made is taking effect. It's good, but it's like drinking molten tar."

Shar laughed. "Yeah, it's heavily fortified. One cup will do me."

Just then, our eleven-year-old nephew James came up to us and tugged his Auntie Sharlene away. "You have *got* to see this game Riley has in his room!" he insisted.

But no sooner had James dragged my sister away than my sister-in-law materialized in her place.

"So," Olivia said, looking bright-eyed and impish, "what's going on with you, Blake?"

"Nothing unusual," I lied. And I could tell she knew it, too, because she slanted me a look that said, *Dude, I've known you for more than a dozen years, don't bullshit me.*

Her actual words were a little gentler. "You just seem to have a lot on your mind. Everything okay at the station?"

"Yeah. Same old, same old."

"With Winston?"

"He's improving every day." That mutt of mine had a spirit that couldn't be easily broken. Thank God. "I'll be taking him into the vet for another checkup early next week, but he's definitely on the mend."

"That's so good to hear," Olivia gushed. Then she went in for the kill. "So, it's about a woman then, right?"

"Um." I tried to gulp down some coffee, but the thick

potency of it caught in my throat and just made me cough.

She lowered her voice, said, "C'mon, Blake," and tugged me to the corner of the kitchen, as far away as possible from the rest of our relatives without creating suspicion. "You can tell me what's really going on."

I studied her face for a moment—her expression was curious but very kind. The courtship she and Derek had a dozen years ago had been very short but, much as I'd always liked Derek's ex, Jaleina, I knew the second I saw him with Olivia that the two of them belonged together. With some people, the connection was obvious.

"Okay, yes," I confessed. "It's about a woman. But—" I paused. "She and I aren't some perfect match. Not like you and my brother. Things with us didn't just fall into place the minute we met. It's been...freakin' weird from the beginning."

Olivia tilted her head and squinted at me. "You think things with Derek and me just 'fell into place' effortlessly? Like there wasn't any work involved?"

I shrugged. I kinda did, yeah, but I got the sense that this wasn't the right answer.

My sister-in-law leaned closer to me and hissed, "Let me make this easy for you—you're *insane* if you think so."

"I've been called worse."

She laughed. "Blake, I know it was a long time ago. You were in college then, and Chance and Chandler were only sixteen when Derek and I got married. But there was a lot of tension. Tons of things your big brother and I had to work through. And not just the fact that I'd been in a serious relationship with someone else before we'd met, and he'd had a fiancée. For the first few years of our marriage, that fact still came up when we had fights."

My jaw dropped. "What? You mean Derek brought it up? He blamed you for breaking up his engagement?"

She shook her head. "No. *I* brought it up. I reminded him that he'd once changed his mind about marrying someone. Someone who was very sweet, and who I'd probably be good friends with if I hadn't messed up her plans for the future." She swallowed. "I was insecure about the whole thing. I thought he might change his mind about me, too, someday. Plus, I was wildly hormonal."

We laughed briefly about that. Olivia had been more than two months pregnant with James on their wedding day, but neither she nor my brother knew it until after the honeymoon.

"Derek felt, and not unjustly, that I didn't completely trust him, and he wrestled with those emotions." She rested her hand on my forearm. "So you see, we might've seemed perfectly matched to other people, but we still had a lot of issues to work through between us."

"But it turned out for the best," I managed to say. "I can't imagine he ever regrets now that he and Jaleina broke things off. You don't think so, do you?"

She shook her head. "No more than I regret breaking up with my boyfriend at the time. I'm just saying that all couples go through rough patches. All couples have to figure out if they're both willing to take a leap of faith. Despite their doubts. Despite their fears."

"Maybe I'm not cut out for that. For being part of a real couple for the long haul. Maybe she's right to have doubts about me. I think what I'm feeling is...love, maybe...or at least the beginning of it. But how the hell can I know for sure, let alone try to convince her?"

"Oh, Blake," Olivia whispered. "You're more than capable of love. You demonstrate your love of your siblings and of your nephews and of me every time you're with us. You're loyal. You show up when we need you. And I remember you with your parents. No one could have cared more. Worked harder to make them comfortable during their final days."

"But that's family. Everyone loves their family."

She shook her head again. "No. Not everyone."

And I remembered too late that, in Olivia's case, she'd had a mother who'd abandoned her and her father when she was a teen. She almost never talked about it, but I knew the pain of that betrayal had never left her.

"Sorry, Olivia."

She waved away my apology. "No worries. You Michaelsens are so bonded to each other that sometimes you don't see that this isn't always the case with the rest of the world. But, anyway, it's not just with family that you show your love. You adore that dog of yours with a fierceness and a wholeheartedness that a woman wants and needs."

I felt my face heat up a little. "Well, for God's sake, don't tell anybody *that*. I'm pretty sure no woman would want me to say, 'Hey, I love you like I love my dog.'"

Olivia grinned. "Only a woman that really knows you, Blake. Then that's the *only* thing she'd want to hear."

~*Vicky*~

This week was never going to end.

Tomorrow night was the Homecoming dance, though. I just had to make it through one more full day and, then, life would get back to normal. It had to, didn't it?

I muttered soothing phrases to myself in French. Me telling me that everything was going to be all right—*tout va bien se passer*—which always seemed to ground me in the present and calm me down. Foreign languages reminded me that the world was larger than just this little corner of Illinois. That what was happening here wasn't happening everywhere. That the universe was bigger than what was going on in my insignificant little life.

I tossed my school bag in the backseat of my car, but I couldn't bring myself to go home just yet. It was October first and a beautiful fall afternoon, approaching evening. The trees were beginning to turn colors. Some much more determinedly than others, I noticed.

Why were some things—and some people—capable of changing more quickly than those around them? Why did some people get over old relationships and jump into new ones more easily than...well, me?

I was pondering this and wandering aimlessly, or so I thought at first. But it turned out I knew exactly where I was going.

The junior high building was just across the street from the high school. I spotted Shar's car from halfway across the parking lot, which meant she was still here. I found myself checking in at the office and walking down to Shar's classroom before I could think twice.

"Hi there, stranger," my friend said when she saw me. "What brings you over to this building, home to crazy junior high teachers and rugrats alike."

"You," I admitted with a smile. "Need any help?" Shar was tacking up a jack-o-lantern border on one of her classroom bulletin boards. It looked like she had stories written by her eighth graders that she planned to display.

"Sure. Grab this edge."

I held one end of the jack-o-lantern border in place while she stapled it securely to the board. When she finished all four sides, she put down her stapler, grinned at me, and said, "What's been going on, Vicky? I know something's up."

I nodded. "Yeah. I haven't wanted to talk about it because—" I hesitated and ran my fingers through my hair to buy time.

"Because?" Shar prompted.

"Because it's about your brother."

"Aw, crap. Has Blake been pestering you again? Do I need to have another talk with him?"

I shook my head. "He hasn't been pestering me. He's— uh—he and I have, um..." I couldn't quite figure out how to say it without just blurting it out. "We've been kind of seeing each other. Casually. *Very* casually, and recently. *Really* recently."

My friend grimaced. "No wonder he looked so cagey this morning. I should've guessed he was back to his old wild behavior." She sighed heavily. "I'm so sorry, Vicky. Has he been impossible to reach now? Since your 'date,' that is?" She said the word like it had air quotes.

"No."

"Has he been pretending that he was getting back together with an ex-girlfriend—a flight attendant named Kimberly, perhaps?"

"What? No."

She snapped her fingers. "Has he been coming up with odd-sounding and entirely fictional illnesses to keep from meeting you when you want to talk?"

"Not yet, Shar. It's, um, really not like that."

"Then, what's it like?"

I took a deep breath and launched into the whole story. How he'd been acting so much like a playboy at first—inappropriately propositioning me and constantly fooling around. Then there was that day of Winston's accident and how our relationship just changed. How we got closer after that. Started talking. And kissing. And having meals together, including our date in Chicago...and then going to my apartment afterward.

Shar stared at me, dumbfounded. "You slept with my brother?"

I nodded.

"And you...enjoyed it?"

I nodded again.

"Oh, my God, Vicky! You know I'm happy for you both, right? And you know I'd talk about all the juicy, sexy details with you if it involved *any* other guy, but with Blake or, really, with any of my brothers—I mean, I just don't think I can—"

"No! I'm definitely *not* sharing those details with you,

Shar. Trust me. That's not what this is about."

She looked relieved. "Okay. So, if things went well between the two of you physically, and if he's not running away for a change, what's the issue?"

"*I'm* the one who's been running away." I told her about the conversation Blake and I had on Sunday. About how he suddenly wanted more than the one-night stand he'd originally claimed to want.

She narrowed her eyes at me. "We're still talking about Blake *Michaelsen,* right? *My* brother? The commitment-phobe?"

I assured her that, yes, we were still discussing the same man.

Shar's comical disbelief disappeared and she turned very serious. "Wait—are you saying you don't have feelings for him? Or are you afraid to get involved with him because of *me?* Because of our friendship or because of the things I'd told you about him?"

"I do have feelings for him, Shar. I don't entirely understand them. But, yes, they're there, and, yes, your warnings about him made me think twice. Even so, I still went ahead with everything this weekend. I was so sure I knew what he wanted. So sure I knew what *I* wanted. But now... Now I have no idea. It scares me to think of really getting involved with someone again. Anyone. Putting my heart out there. I can't deny that I'm drawn to Blake, but he and I are so different. It would be much easier to just let things drift between us. For this to be the fling it was supposed to be." I paused. *"Est-ce que ça vaut la peine de lutter pour l'amour?"* I murmured.

"What's that mean?" my friend asked.

"Is love worth fighting for?" I said.

She squeezed her eyes shut. "Oh, Vicky, that's the wrong question."

"Why?"

"Love is *always* worth fighting for. But that's not where

you're at in your relationship with my dorky brother. You're at that place of uncertainty. Where there's no guarantee of anything, for either of you yet. So the question is whether or not you're even willing to risk it. If the *possibility* of love is worth attempting."

She was right, and I knew it the moment she spoke. Unlike me, Shar had been married and divorced. She'd risked big, and she'd lost. She wasn't over the pain of that, and I didn't blame her.

"I'm scared of what I'm feeling," I confessed. "Terrified, actually."

"I know you are. And, from everything you've told me and from the shell-shocked expression on my brother's face this morning, he is, too." She buried her head in her palms. "I feel so damn guilty. I'm his sister, and I love him. I'm your friend, and I adore you. But I had no idea you two might become an actual couple. You were both standing right in front of me, and I didn't see how well it might work until just now."

"You can't blame yourself for this—"

"Yes, I can. How could I be so blind? I interfered in the worst way possible. You trusted me to be honest when I told you about Blake's typical relationship behavior. And everything I said may have been true in the past or with other women but, with *you,* he's not necessarily the same guy."

I reminded her of the provocative things he'd spouted off in my classroom, at the park, and in other places around Mirabelle Harbor.

"Yeah, but you might have interpreted his intentions differently or reacted by being less frustrated with him if I hadn't prejudiced you against him. I fanned the flames of your distrust." She shook her head. "And I told you only about his annoying traits. Granted, there are many of those, but Blake's also got a huge heart. You don't know how loyal he can be to the people he loves. How generous. He has at least as many good qualities as irritating ones, and now I feel as though I've not only misled you, but I've also betrayed him."

My friend had tears in her eyes. I knew she genuinely meant every word she said, but I also felt her sense of accountability here had gone too far.

"Shar, no. You need to stop thinking this way. Please. You're not responsible for our decisions. Not Blake's, and definitely not mine. Don't forget, I *chose* to sleep with him, despite all of your warnings. You can't be held accountable for that any more than you can for any other choice I've ever made. You're intensely involved in the lives of the people you care about but, let's be honest, while we all love you and value your opinion, you're not *that* powerful."

She finally laughed. "Okay. Fair enough. So then, what can I do? How can I help you now?"

Until this very second, I hadn't known what the answer to that question might be. But once Shar's words were in the air between us, it came to me.

"There *is* something you can explain, which, maybe, will help me understand your brother a bit better."

"Shoot," she said.

"What's the deal with him not liking romance?"

Shar pointed to a student chair. "Have a seat. And get comfortable. This is gonna take a while."

CHAPTER THIRTEEN

~*Vicky*~

I was trying to be a supportive teacher and watch the Homecoming football game the following night. I cheered on the Mirabelle Harbor Hawks to the best of my ability as they attempted to crush the Highbury Park Panthers. And our team won—narrowly, by a field goal—in a 24 to 21 victory.

But, obviously, my mind wasn't on the game.

I'd slipped away multiple times during the second half to check on the teens busily decorating the gym and on the parent chaperones who'd graciously agreed to help out at the dance tonight. And, of course, I was always keeping an eye out for Blake, who arrived just when we'd asked him to (at the start of the fourth quarter) and made quick work of setting up his equipment.

I waved to him when he walked through the gym doors. He acknowledged me with a wave in return. But that was all.

Our pattern of interaction had been disrupted and was now a very strange and awkward thing. I'd gotten used to him chasing me and cajoling me into doing things. My role until recently had been to parry his advances and, occasional, agree to be swayed by one of his suggestions. Which made his distant behavior this week all the more odd.

I couldn't believe how much I'd found myself missing him. His flirtatiousness had been flattering, I had to admit. And, sure, his overt sexual innuendos had been equal parts annoying and amusing, but they were always memorable. If I were to be completely honest with myself, though, what I really missed was the unique combination of qualities that made up the man himself. Blake might not be perfect, but he wasn't what anyone would consider ordinary.

Yesterday, in Shar's classroom, she'd responded to something about her brother that I'd long wondered: If his deep resistance to romance was because he'd been badly hurt in love.

The answer was no.

But his sister explained that he was far more sensitive, far more empathetic to others than most people realized. He'd witnessed too many situations where people he cared about had been hurt by love or, more precisely, by the loss of it.

"He has such a fear of being vulnerable," Shar had said. "It's going to be incredibly difficult for him to overcome that. His internal walls are a mile high. But once somebody manages to worm their way into his heart, they're there to stay."

She also said something else that I took to be as much of a friendly warning as it was advice.

"Blake's not necessarily an easy choice for a boyfriend. Not only isn't he the romantic White Knight type, he doesn't *want* to be. Whomever he's with would need to want the real man, flaws and all. And she'd probably need to prove that to him. He won't settle for anything less. So, Vicky, if you choose him, you need to pick him with your eyes wide open. And if you decide you *don't* want to be with him, please do him the kindness of not dragging things out. Blake's always been a pull-the-bandage-off-fast kind of guy."

As I watched Blake adjusting his DJ equipment across the gym, I couldn't get his sister's words out of my mind. There was something different about him tonight that I couldn't quite put my finger on. An underlying seriousness despite his usual friendly exterior.

I observed the way he was interacting with the other people in the gym. A rotating series of parent chaperones came up to him to shake his hand and, no doubt, tell Blake how much they enjoyed listening to him on the radio.

However, even though a couple of those parents were very attractive single moms, I could tell he wasn't flirting with them. There was an air of detachment about him that I could recognize even across the room.

And there were teenagers zooming around us everywhere. Every member of the Homecoming committee and a handful of their friends also stopped by to welcome Blake and to chat with him.

He grinned at them all, took time to answer their questions, and seemed to regard them with gentle amusement but, as he did with the parents, he kept a cool distance. Like he was politely marking time until he could go home.

I finally spotted a gap when he had no visitors, and walked up to him.

"Hi, Blake. Thanks for getting here early." I glanced at the equipment in front of him. "It looks like you already have everything set up."

He nodded briefly and busied himself connecting some kind of cable to the sound system. "Just about," he said.

With so much of the music being organized digitally, there weren't many things that needed prepping. But whether it was necessary or not, Blake seemed to find tasks to keep him occupied while I was standing there. I knew an avoidance technique when I saw one.

I took a step back and just said, "Well, if you need anything during the dance, please let me know." As I started to walk away, though, he called me back.

"Vicky," he said, finally meeting my gaze. Then, with a hoarse whisper, "It's good to see you. You look really nice tonight."

I'd chosen my dress—a violet-colored, tea-length gown—with Blake in mind. I didn't know why, but I just knew it would be a color he'd like. Not that I was going to tell him that.

"Thank you," I said. "So do you."

Actually, "nice" was a woefully poor descriptor. Rather, he looked dashing in his dark-gray dress pants, white button-up shirt, black sports jacket, and designer tie—one that had little footballs all over it. He caught me staring at it and half grinned.

"Figured this would be appropriate, given the game and all," he said.

I was about to say something light and unimportant in response, like how the clothing we wore matched the purple and black dance theme colors the kids had chosen, really just for the purpose of keeping our conversation going. But Blake abruptly grabbed his keys and said, "Hey, I forgot something in the van. Gotta run out there. Hope you'll enjoy the music tonight." And he all but sprinted out of the gym.

If that wasn't an obvious sign of dismissal, I didn't know what was.

When the dance began a half hour later, I was kept busy by the committee kids and their flurry of last-minute questions. Heath and Alexis needed help finding stronger tape when the masking tape they'd used to hang up Heath's "Tribute to the Eighties" mural on the wall wasn't holding. Though, once that last task of theirs was complete, they hugged each other and started to dancing right in front of it to the sounds of Madonna's "Crazy for You." I loved seeing their youthful, hopeful smiles.

Also out on the dance floor, I spotted Carson and Amanda, who'd arrived together just a few minutes earlier. Whatever he'd said to her had her laughing harder than I'd ever seen her. This alone made my heart soar. They were a pair that deserved some happy memories.

Matt, as the junior class president, had been one of the most popular kids in his grade from elementary school on. And while he could have asked any available girl in the gym to dance with him (and most would have jumped at the chance), Matt spent the first full hour of the dance hovering around Blake, inquiring about the music, and probably asking a gazillion questions about life as a radio DJ.

Blake had warmly welcomed everyone to the Homecoming dance and, periodically, would unleash his considerable charm on the crowd and announce a new set of songs. When not talking with his sexy voice into the mic, he chatted with Matt, showed him how to work the equipment, and looked pleased to have someone to keep him company.

Stephanie, head of the committee and one of the world's most responsible teenagers, buzzed between the refreshments table, the picture station, and me, particularly when she felt the need to report on something.

"We're almost out of plastic cups for the soda," she said, breathless from her jog across the gym. "Should I run to the store quick and buy more?"

"No, don't leave the party," I said. "Let me check the foreign language office for you. We may have some extra paper and plastic products left over from last year's Fête. You just keep an eye on things here."

She nodded gratefully. "*Merci beaucoup,* Mademoiselle."

Blake, who'd been looking with riveted attention at Matt and, occasionally, at anybody else in the room who wasn't me, suddenly shot me a curious glance as I strode past him and toward the gym doors. I could feel his gaze following me. Could almost hear him questioning my departure.

For someone who'd spent more than half of the event studiously avoiding me, this struck me as odd. I couldn't imagine why he'd care where I went if he so desperately didn't want to even look at me, let alone talk to me.

But, whatever his reasoning, when I returned to the gym with the extra cups, it seemed as though Blake's eyes hadn't left the door. Matt was still standing beside him, still yakking away, but Blake was staring directly at me, as if he'd been waiting for my return.

After that, he tracked my every move. Watched as I brought the plastic cups to the refreshments table. Studied me as I spoke briefly with Stephanie.

It wasn't until after I'd stepped away from the drinks and treats that Blake left his DJ post for the first time. But did he come to talk with me? No. He went to the refreshments table and talked with everyone there. He said a few things to Stephanie, too. Complimented her, I could tell, because she blushed prettily and tried to shrug off his words.

Then he poured two cups of soda and strode over in my direction...but, again, not to me. He stopped and offered the drinks to a couple of chaperones.

I watched him repeat this exercise several times. Going to the refreshments table. Pouring some sodas. Handing them out to chaperones in the general vicinity. It was, I had to admit, an incredibly thoughtful gesture. Maybe that was why he was so interested when I left the gym and returned with the plastic cups. Maybe it wasn't about me at all. He just knew there were a lot of thirsty parent volunteers in the room.

Then he was back at the DJ station, continuing his conversation with Matt and pointing out some notes to him that were printed on sheets of white paper.

A few minutes later, Blake clicked on his mic and addressed the crowd. "Let's hear it once again for the Mirabelle Harbor Hawks! What a great game tonight."

The students in attendance went wild with their cheers.

When the commotion died down to a low roar, Blake added, "I wanted to give a shout out to the Homecoming committee. They've done such an awesome job organizing the dance tonight, raising money for the food and decorations, and making sure everything would run smoothly. Let's show our appreciation to Stephanie Little, Alexis Cho, Heath Murray, and my man up here—Matt Rosatti!"

A deafening round of applause followed.

"Matt's gonna help me spin this next tune," Blake continued. "It goes out to all of the football players on the team who fought so hard on the field tonight."

More loud applause, and it only grew louder when Matt pressed a few buttons and Queen's "We Are the Champions" began to play. That song hadn't been on Blake's original playlist, but it certainly fit the mood of the night.

He caught my eye the moment the chorus started, and he deliberately held my gaze. Without breaking our eye contact, he whispered a few words to Matt and then waded through a sea of singing teens to where I was standing.

Finally.

"Before you chew me out about this," he said with more than a hint of defensiveness, "I know I'm deviating from the approved playlist. I realize this isn't a love song. That it's not even from the Eighties. It came out in 1977, but Freddie Mercury's voice rocks, and—"

"And it's an excellent choice," I interrupted. "I'm not arguing with you about the music, Blake. You've done a fabulous job tonight, and the kids are having the best time."

"So I don't have to plead my case?"

"Not about the song," I said.

A smile tugged at his lips. "Good."

"And it was really sweet of you to recognize the students on the committee, not just the football players." I nodded toward Matt. "I think you've earned yourself a faithful assistant, too, whenever you might need one."

"He's a terrific kid," Blake said. "Funny as hell. I've never seen anybody get so excited about pressing a few buttons."

"He looks up to you, Blake. It's been wonderful to see him coming out of his shell again this fall, especially after the past two years."

"Why? What happened?"

I realized Blake didn't know the background of the students the way I did. "Matt's parents got divorced during his freshman year, and his dad took off to Seattle. The guy rarely comes back and doesn't make much time to spend with his son when he goes there. It's been really hard on Matt, and he's struggled a lot with his self image during high school."

Blake looked at me with surprise. "I had no idea. He comes across as so confident."

"Yeah. He's always been a popular kid with his peers, and he manages to hide his insecurities well. He dropped French this year, but he was in my class for his first two years. The students write personal essays for me in their journals. They're just short paragraphs, but the kids know they're private and that I don't share them with anyone else. In that forum, Matt was always very honest about his feelings."

"Some kids have to deal with so much," Blake murmured.

"Oh, I know." I glanced around the gym until I spotted Amanda and Carson. I surreptitiously pointed them out to

Blake. "Those two have had to overcome a lot as well. It's been a joy to see them find each other and carve out a little normal teenage fun, despite some very serious issues."

"I'm almost afraid to ask—what kind of issues?"

This was common knowledge at the high school but, again, not something Blake would necessarily know unless he was acquainted with the families. I motioned Blake closer. "Health issues. Amanda started high school wearing a wig. She'd been diagnosed with cancer in eighth grade and spent the summer before her freshman year going through sixteen weeks of chemotherapy."

Blake blinked at me. "Oh, no. That's—that's—" He didn't finish. He just shook his head and stared at the girl with the short blond hair who was still twirling in Carson's arms. "But she's okay now?"

"For now, yes. Thank goodness. The cancer is in remission, but Amanda still misses a lot of school because of doctor appointments," I said. "Carson goofs off in class more than most of the kids, but I stopped getting mad at him when I realized why. He was trying so hard to make her laugh."

Just talking about this made me a little more emotional than I liked to admit but, although Blake had always been good with the kids, I wanted him to understand why I cared so much about them. I wanted him to realize that they all had stories. That, despite everything that might be going on in their lives, they were still so hopeful. So optimistic. They were part of what kept me wishing for happily ever afters.

I brushed away a tear that had escaped and saw Blake studying the young couple on the dance floor with new eyes.

"If you want to know the truth," I said, "I don't think Carson even likes French. But he's stuck with it these last couple of years because of her."

Blake exhaled slowly and nodded. He motioned toward Alexis and Heath, who were slow dancing to the song that

Matt had been put in charge of playing next—Cyndi Lauper's "Time After Time." He asked, "What about them?"

"No sad stories that I know of, but Heath was always a really quiet boy. Crazy talented in art, just not the strongest student when it came to the core curricular subjects. Alexis is his complete opposite. Very verbal. Very much of a high achiever in school. Until recently, they ran in totally different circles."

"Did they meet because of the Homecoming committee?"

"I'm pretty sure they knew who each other was before, but I don't know if they'd ever really spoken until Stephanie roped them both into joining the committee," I said. "I more than suspect that Heath had a crush on Alexis from afar, but I don't think he would have acted on it and asked her to be his date at the dance if she hadn't openly admired his artwork. I was proud of her for recognizing his gifts, especially since they're so different from her own. And I was proud of him, too, for being courageous and stepping out of his comfort zone."

"That's sweet," Blake said. "And kinda romantic."

I laughed. "It is. It takes a lot to get you to appreciate that, doesn't it?"

He shrugged, but he was smiling. "My parents met the same way. Back in high school. They had such a classic love story and were together for decades. Always faithful to each other—at least as far as I know—and they managed to raise five kids. If they were still alive, they would've been married forty-two years this Christmas."

Shar had told me how affected Blake had been by the loss of their parents. How painful it was for them all to watch their mother suffer after the passing of their father, but that Blake had taken it especially hard. "You must miss them a lot," I said.

"I do. I even miss their parental advice," he confessed.

"There are tons of things I'd love to ask them both now that I wasn't ready to know when they were here."

"Yeah?" I left my question open-ended. Maybe he'd want to tell me. Maybe he wouldn't.

After a long moment, he added, "About relationships mostly. Hell, about a lot of life's most important things." He nodded toward Stephanie, who was still busying herself with the refreshments table and making sure everything was perfect. As usual, she was being ever vigilant and not taking any time for herself, even though the dance was running as smoothly as it could be by now. "What's her story?"

"High achiever. Perfectionist. Very attentive but demanding parents. They care about her and they show their love, but their expectations are probably overwhelming. Or they would be to someone who was less capable than Stephanie is. I tell her what a wonderful job she's doing whenever possible. I try to reassure her that she doesn't need to worry so much. But I don't know if anything I'm saying is sinking in. She's a lot like me when I was in high school," I admitted with a laugh. "Works hard. Plays it safe."

Blake leaned in and nudged me with his shoulder. "I was so afraid of girls like you in high school." He paused. "Still am a little intimidated, actually."

"Why?"

He slanted me a sideways glance. "Your type always seemed to know what you were doing. Knew where you were going. I was almost always blundering my way around—lost and trying like hell not to show it. And if nothing else that I did could distract everyone's attention away from how scared I was, I'd pick a fight." He winked at me. "Worked every time."

"Guess we're pretty different from each other, huh?"

"Yep. Though some people say opposites attract," he murmured. He didn't give me a chance to reply to this statement, nor did he let on if he was one of the people who believed it. He just pointed at the sound equipment. "Look, I've got to get back to being a DJ for a little while. Matt's already up to the Whitesnake tune. He's gonna run into a music gap in a sec. So—" He semi-smiled at me. "Maybe we'll talk later?"

"Yeah," I managed.

As he rushed away, I thought about our many conversations. Some had been silly, sure, but there had been a few, like this one, that were totally lacking in pretense. Why did it take me hurting him and making it clear to him that we probably shouldn't be together for all the feelings I'd tried to ignore about the man to come rushing in?

His personality and mine were stunningly different— that was undeniable. But he had gifts, skills, traits, and tons of good qualities that I could learn from and appreciate. I tried to imagine him as a high-school kid. As a student in some teacher's class. He must have been such a smart ass as a teen, and I knew he'd been aggressive. A fighter. But I'd never thought about *why*. About what he'd been seeking during those adolescent years. About what he'd been afraid of. These tiny glimpses into his past were telling.

It occurred to me, watching him at the DJ station with Matt, that the two of them may have bonded so quickly because they both shared the experience of having a very public and well-liked veneer, but they both also had insecurities and confidence issues underneath that façade. Both wanted to excel at something. Discover a place where they could really belong. And, despite their popularity, neither of them had an easy time finding true acceptance.

Then again, maybe none of us ever fully resolved whatever issues we'd grappled with as teens. Perhaps it had been my own issues—just as much as Blake's—that had been driving a wedge between us. Maybe a part of me was still running from my high-school self. Hoping I could finally get a romantic relationship right.

~*Blake*~

The whole time Whitesnake's "Is This Love?" was playing, all I could think about was how soon I could get back to standing next to Vicky. Just talking with her. Hell, just *being* with her.

I kept wishing I'd have a familiar reaction to fall back on. One that was all about wanting the release of sex or desiring the mind-numbing intoxication of flirtation and foreplay.

But my desire for her wasn't just a physical or a psychological need. It was both. And it was *more*.

"Thanks for trusting me to do that set," Matt said, his voice wistful. "It was really cool getting to run things over here for a few minutes."

"Glad you liked it. Wanna do another one in a bit?"

"Yeah!"

He was so enthusiastic, I had to laugh. "You know, if by the end of the night you still think this is fun, you're welcome to come to the radio station sometime. I could show you the ropes, and you can see if it's a career option you'd like to consider."

He looked at me with brown eyes so huge and surprised that I thought he might not speak. Then, "Oh, my God. *Really?*"

"Absolutely. I'd love to have you visit for an afternoon. Maybe one of my weekend shifts, so it doesn't interfere with your classes, eh?"

"Anytime. Just say when. I am so there!"

"Good. Leave me your email. I'll check the schedule next week and message you with a few possible dates." I glanced at my watch. Only a half hour left of the dance before we had to wrap up. "So, Matt, is Stephanie still hanging out by the refreshments table?" I knew she was. I just wanted him to look over there while I got the next set ready.

"Yep," he said.

I couldn't get Vicky's words about the students out of my head. And though I was the last person on Earth who should ever play matchmaker, I'd lived with Shar for long enough to know a good opportunity to pair up two people when I saw one.

"Any sodas, cookies, and chips still on the table?" I asked him.

Matt said there were. "Want me to get you something?"

"Not me," I replied. "*You.* You should take a break. Grab a Coke. Chat with Stephanie for a few minutes. Maybe dance to a little David Bowie." I pointed to the song list. "Let's Dance" was coming up soon. "She's a pretty cool girl, don't you think?"

"Stephanie?" he said. "Uh, yeah. She's also really smart."

"Well, that's not a bad thing, is it?"

He shook his head.

"And she's cute, too, right?"

Matt had fair skin and couldn't hide his blush. "Yeah." He glanced between her and me, considering what I was not-so-subtly suggesting.

"You should celebrate the night," I added. "You two were half of the crew that created it, after all."

"We were only one-third of the crew," Matt shot back, proving he was adept at math. "We couldn't have done it without you and Mademoiselle."

"Thanks," I said. "Nice of you to say. More true of your teacher than of me, though. But I've got a little something planned for her."

The kid raised his eyebrows and looked intrigued. "Really? Oooh. I think maybe you like—"

"Stop thinking, Matt," I commanded, turning him around and pointing him in the direction of the refreshments. "Go eat something, drink something, chat with Stephanie, dance. I'll call you back here before the end of the night and you can spin the final set. Deal?"

He grinned. "Deal." And he was off.

From across the gym, I could see Vicky checking in with a few adult chaperones, but her eyes never strayed far from her favorite students. When she spotted Matt and Stephanie talking to each other, she looked pleased. And when the Bowie song started to play and those two teens began to dance, her face lit up like holiday lights on a tree.

She looked over at me, smiling. I smiled back. I loved seeing her so happy.

Hearing the stories she told me about the kids damn near brought tears to my eyes. Maybe I was just getting sentimental in my old age—sappy song lyrics and touching stories were starting to get to me in a way they never used to. I'd read that this could happen. That being forced to confront our mortality as we got older made most people more emotional. I just never thought I'd be one of them. Turned out, there'd been a lot of firsts since I'd met Vicky.

But, in any case, I truly understood something about her now. She was a romantic not because she was blind to the real world...but because she *wasn't*. Because of her students and what she saw in them. Because she wasn't capable of wishing them anything but the best for their future, no matter what had transpired in their past.

I wanted her to feel honored and treasured, too. To know how much I admired and appreciated her, even if I only had tonight to tell her.

Maybe we didn't stand a chance in Hades of making an actual relationship work, no matter what Olivia said. Maybe life had made me too cynical, and it had made Vicky too soft. But if we were ever going to get to know each other, I'd have to show her that I could be more open. More honest. Even marginally more heroic.

And if anyone in the world deserved a grand romantic

gesture at a Homecoming dance, it was Vicky Bernier.

So, once I'd given Matt and Stephanie the opportunity to rock out to a handful of songs, and I'd finished the current set of tunes, I prepped the final musical rotation—choosing the song order carefully. Then I took a deep breath and clicked on my mic.

"The clock is going to strike midnight soon, but before we go, it's time to say thanks to all the teachers and parent chaperones who volunteered here tonight."

I waited for the clapping to die down before I continued.

"And I think we all know Mademoiselle Vicky Bernier deserves a special round of applause. Not only is she an incredible teacher and a fearless staff advisor to the Homecoming committee, but I've never met anyone so beautiful—inside and out."

There, I'd said it. A moment of stunned silence followed as the crowd digested what I'd just confessed. Then there was a wild burst of cheering and whistling.

Vicky looked over at me in total surprise before giving an embarrassed shrug and shaking her head, as if she wasn't completely deserving of the compliments and all of this attention. I disagreed. She deserved them and was about to get more.

"I never thought I'd ever feel this way about somebody," I said. "But Vicky is so smart, so kind, and such a good friend, especially when she knew I needed one." I smiled at her from half a packed gym away, willing her to feel the sincerity of my words. "And despite the fact that she's one of those 'cat' people—" The kids and the adults laughed. "She's also really good with my dog. She's ethical, dedicated, hardworking, and so sweet. You're all lucky to have her at your school. And I know I'm a better man just for having met her."

I paused again, watching her take in my comments and waiting for what I said to fully sink in. It was, for a minute, as if it were just the two of us alone in the cavernous room. Just one hopeful guy talking to his belle of the ball, and praying she wouldn't disappear the second the clock struck twelve.

"Earlier in the evening," I said to everyone, "she told me to let her know if I needed anything. Well, I do. And I've got my fingers crossed that she won't shoot me down in front of most of the school, but I can't let the night end without asking her to dance with me. Vicky—will you?" I addressed her directly. "*You* are what I need."

A shaft of light caught her face, and I could see that tears were streaming down her cheeks. She brushed them away, though, and nodded at me.

Relief flooded my body, and I broke into a grin. "Thank you," I said into the mic. And then, "If my assistant Matt could come up here and help me out with this final set, I'd appreciate it."

The kid materialized beside me before I'd even finished the sentence.

"Way to go, man!" he whispered as he took over the DJ station with some expertise now.

"Thanks, Matt," I said. "Wish me luck."

"Luck."

Then, on my nod, he pressed the button to start the next song. REO Speedwagon's "Can't Fight This Feeling" started to play. I walked over to stand in front of Vicky and held my hand out to her.

She took it, and I pulled her into my arms.

Almost everyone who'd been dancing before just stood to the side and watched until we'd danced the first verse alone. Then, gradually, the floor started filling up with teen couples and we were surrounded by the buoyancy of young love.

Only once the first chorus had ended and fewer people were staring at us did Vicky speak. "That was a really slick move, Blake." She glanced up at me with a serious expression. "You had to know that I'd never say no to you in front of all the kids."

I stopped in place, my arms still encircling her but no part of me was moving except for my heart, which had plummeted to my toes. "So, you're saying you don't want to dance with me after all?"

"No." She rolled her eyes and broke into a huge smile. "I'm *not* saying that. I'm simply acknowledging what a good strategist you are."

Okay. She was teasing me. I could handle that. I could give as good as I got. Especially now that my heart was starting to make the slow journey back up to my chest again.

I raised one eyebrow and forced a smirk at her. "Why, that's an awfully cynical comment coming from an alleged romantic like *you*, Mademoiselle."

She feigned an uninterested shrug, but I knew she cared about whatever I'd say next more than she was letting on. Just watching her trying so hard not to let herself get carried away by the fairytale-like fantasy of this moment was cute. And a little heartbreaking.

A part of me wanted to continue joking with her. But, though it would be easy to banter, I couldn't bring myself to let even a tiny part of her think that what I'd said tonight was a *strategy* of mine.

I leaned down to whisper in her ear. "I'm not playing you, Vicky. You don't have to protect yourself from me, okay? I'm being sincere. *Je t'aime*, Mademoiselle."

She swallowed hard and squinted at me. "You love me?" she whispered back, incredulous. "No, you don't."

"*Oui*, I do," I countered. "Somehow, you just snuck into my heart and kind of took it over. I'm not going anywhere so, seriously, you're stuck with me."

I wasn't sure if this statement worried her more than elated her, but she bit her lip and stared at me for a long time, contemplating.

"I mean it," I said, refusing to start dancing again until she believed me on this.

Finally, she nodded. "Shar said you were like that."

It was my turn to stare in shock at her. "*Shar* said?"

"Yeah. I had a long talk with her about you yesterday." She blushed, and I could only guess at the way that conversation must have gone.

My concern must have shown because Vicky shook her head and said, "Don't worry. It was all good."

"Let me just make sure I understand this. You told my sister about us? I thought you didn't want her to know that we—"

"I didn't tell her *everything,* Blake. But, yes. She knows a lot about our relationship now. I had to talk to somebody who cares about you as much as I do. I hope you don't mind that I—"

I kissed her.

Right there in the middle of the high-school gym. With teens and teachers and parents watching. I didn't care who saw us.

And Vicky kissed me back. A promise, I hoped, of what was yet to come.

When we broke apart, I was vaguely aware of a bunch of people clapping and pointing at us, of Glass Tiger singing "I Will Be There," as the last set of the Eighties music was winding down, and of Vicky looking at me with a dazed expression on her beautiful face. We both had professional tasks to attend to before the night was over, but I wanted to be sure she knew I didn't intend to go home tonight without her.

"I have to load up the van and return the equipment to the station," I warned her.

"And I have to help the committee with the clean up and lock the gym once everyone is gone," she said.

"Meet at my place afterward?" I suggested.

"We'll see," she replied noncommittally. But she added

a saucy wink that left me feeling hopeful.

I let Matt give the final announcement of the night. "For the last song," he said exuberantly into the mic, "here's something fast and fun to send you home!" The opening strains of Modern English's "I Melt with You" began to play and the energy level in the gym, which was already high, shot to the ceiling.

I thanked Matt again for his help and sent him on his way. Without even any additional encouragement from me, I saw him seek out Stephanie and spend the last dance bopping around the room with her, both of them laughing as their retro night came to an end.

After the goodbyes were said to the crowd and the lights were turned back on, the clearing out/cleaning up process began. It was nearly one a.m. before the last of the students and chaperones trudged home. My equipment was already stashed in the van, but I couldn't bring myself to leave until I knew for sure what Vicky was going to do next.

She came up to me, keys jangling. There were just the two of us left. "I just locked the gym doors," she announced.

"With us still inside?"

"Yes." And she pressed a finger to my chest and pushed me backward, with no effort at all on her part, until I was up against one of the gym's padded walls. "Kiss me," she demanded.

I wanted to do far, far more than that, but I complied at once. After running my tongue along her bottom lip, I sucked on it and then drew her into me. I stroked her legs through the fabric before finally lifting the hem of her dress and skimming my fingertips against the smooth skin of her thighs. When I reached her panties, I hooked my thumbs on the elastic and was about to pull them down, but an unexpected bolt of commonsense shot through me.

"If we get caught, you'll be fired," I felt compelled to

mention.

"That's right." She playfully tugged at my belt. "So, we *can't* get caught."

I chuckled. I had to be *crazy* about this woman or I would never had said the words I heard coming out of my mouth. "But I don't want to be the one responsible for you losing your job. We should at least get off school property, don't you think?"

She sighed, but then looked at me speculatively. "Well, I do have this fantasy of us at the radio station," she began. "In your booth..."

I groaned. Desire was addling my brain. I could picture us in my booth. So. Damn. Clearly. Hell, I'd pictured it many times before. In considerable detail.

But this thing with Vicky wasn't a fling, and it would be an inauspicious start to our relationship if I were to get busted as well. I told her this.

She nodded, taking it in, while all the time still pressing against me and touching me and, essentially, driving me insane with longing. I could barely breathe from the enticing scent of her. From wanting her so much.

"Then it's going to have to be the van," she concluded.

"The radio station van?"

"Is there another one that I don't know about?"

Swear to God, this woman was going to be the death of me. "Vicky, you have *no idea* how turned on I am by these suggestions of yours," I ground out. "But the van is a very cramped space. There's a bunch of sound equipment already in there. The floor is dirty, hard, cold. You deserve—"

"—to do something a little less safe for a change," she finished for me, which was not the way I would have ended that sentence. But, hey, I could only resist for so long. Especially when she added, "I've got a thick blanket in the trunk of my car that we could spread out on the floor. And aren't the back windows of the van tinted?" She grinned wickedly. "We can park somewhere deserted. Turn on the music, maybe. I'm sure you've got AC/DC's 'You Shook Me All Night Long' on a playlist somewhere in that van, right?"

"I see you've put some thought into this scenario, haven't you?" I said, completely unable to disguise my awe and willingness to go along with every single proposal she had.

"I have," she admitted. "And I think it's going to play out exactly as I've imagined." She paused. "But even if it doesn't, I don't care. I'm in this for a lot longer than tonight. Because...I've been falling in love with you, too, Blake, and I want us to give this a real chance of working."

I didn't think it was possible to feel happier than I already was, and I didn't bother to try to dissuade her from the van idea. We could make it work. The woman knew what she wanted, and I was going to give it to her. With pleasure.

"Okay," I said decisively. "It's a plan. But fair is fair. We'll say it's lady's choice tonight, but I get to choose next."

She looked intrigued. "You have something raunchy in mind?"

"Something a little more surprising than that, Mademoiselle," I confessed, but I wouldn't tell her what it was.

Instead, I kissed her again and, as I let her lead me out of the gym, I thought to myself, *Something romantic.*

CHAPTER FOURTEEN

~Blake~

After the couple of hours we'd spent in the van (which we'd parked in the darkest corner of the Eastman Field parking lot), I knew I'd never be able to drive that vehicle anywhere ever again without remembering Homecoming night and grinning like a fool.

The hours that followed were kind of fuzzy, just because I was so damn exhausted. But it was a *very good* kind of exhausted. All I knew for sure was that I didn't want to part with Vicky, not even for a few hours. So, she helped me return the equipment to the radio station (finally), and then she came over to my apartment.

Winston perked up when he saw her. What could I say? My mutt had good taste. We took him out for a quick walk and then all three of us crashed on my bed for the night.

Hours later, over scrambled eggs and coffee, I said, "So, I've got a proposition for you."

Her eyes lit up. "You figured out a time when we can do it in the LOVE FM booth?"

I laughed. "Not that kind of proposition."

"Ah, bummer."

She was wearing an old red t-shirt of mine, which came down to the middle of her thighs, and she looked adorable in it. I walked over to where she was leaning against the kitchen counter and yanked on one of the sleeves until I'd reeled her toward me.

"I'll work on your request," I said, wrapping my arms around her and pecking a kiss on her nose. "I promise. But what I was thinking involves a different kind of planning."

She traced a pattern of swirls on my back with her fingertips. "I'm listening."

She wasn't really, but she would be. Soon.

"Didn't you say you had parent/teacher conferences at the end of this week?"

"Yes. Our conferences are Thursday afternoon and evening with more on Friday morning. Technically, we're supposed to be out of the building by noon on Friday, though, and we have an incentive to finish up by then because of the long Columbus Day weekend that follows."

That was what I was hoping to hear. Three and a half days wasn't a *lot* of time, but it should be just enough for what I had in mind.

"Great," I said. "So, is your passport still valid?"

~*Vicky*~

Blake could try to deny it all he wanted, but no one who wasn't at least a *little* romantic at heart would have been able to concoct a getaway like this.

"You want to go to Montreal over Columbus Day weekend?" I said when he pulled out this Quebec guidebook he'd gotten and started pointing out sites.

"I think I'd like us to spend more time there than that," he said thoughtfully. "There are a lot of cool places to visit in Quebec City, too, and the surrounding areas. But Montreal is doable in under four days and there are direct flights from Chicago. See?"

He flipped open his laptop and rattled off departure and arrival times. "Think of it as a scouting expedition," he added. "We can maybe make a road trip back later, in the summer, but this would be a really good introduction for me and a *Québécois* refresher course for you. What do you say?"

After staring at him, speechless, for about ten seconds, what I said was..."Let's go!"

Which was how we ended up zooming down Mirabelle Harbor's Main Street at 12:03 p.m. on Friday afternoon.

Our carry-on bags were in the backseat of Blake's car. Our tickets were purchased and our seats were confirmed. Excitement was high.

Until we heard the police sirens behind us and saw the flashing lights.

"Shit," Blake said.

He pulled over, sighed heavily, and rolled down his window. "I wasn't going *that* far above the speed limit," he muttered, just before the officer sidled up to his door.

"Why am I not surprised it's *you* behind the wheel, Blake?" the police officer said.

"T? I mean, *Officer* T?" Blake said. "Dude, you know my car. I wasn't going too fast—"

"Terrance Ryland," the guy said to me. Then, to Blake, "Yes, you were. Twelve miles above the speed limit to be exact. You haven't been drinking, have you?"

"What? No!" Blake said emphatically.

I recognized the cop from that night when Blake got into the fight in front of Max's. There was a solemnity in his dark eyes, but it was softened by a hint of amusement at the corners of his mouth. I got the sense that he was enjoying seeing Blake squirm a little.

"We have to catch a flight this afternoon," Blake explained with an exaggeratedly patient tone. "And traffic to O'Hare can be fierce before a holiday weekend."

The officer raised a disbelieving brow. "You're taking a trip with *him?*" he said to me.

"Yes," I replied.

"Willingly?" the cop asked.

"T!" Blake erupted. *"Really?"*

I laughed. "Absolutely," I said. "And, hi. My name is Vicky Bernier."

Terrance grinned at me. "Lovely to meet you, Vicky." But Blake just looked increasingly irritated, especially when the cop said to him, "Driver's license and insurance registration, please."

"You *know* who I am," Blake retorted but, nevertheless, he fished out his license and insurance card.

The officer pulled out his notepad and scribbled something down on it. He returned the cards to Blake but, with the sheet of paper, he reached through the open window and across the driver's seat and handed that to me. "Keep a close eye on him, Vicky. He can be a wild one." Then he clapped Blake's shoulder with his large palm and said, "See you around, man. And, oh, if I catch you speeding again on my watch, you'll regret it."

Blake rolled his eyes as Terrance sauntered back to his police vehicle, honked at us once, and then drove away. Once the cop was gone, I could tell Blake was finally starting to see the humor in his buddy's traffic stop.

"So, you guys have been friends for a long time?" I guessed.

"Forever," Blake admitted. "Early elementary school." He looked curiously at the sheet of paper Terrance had given me. "That's not a ticket, is it?"

I shook my head. "It says 'Warning' at the top, though, and then: 'Have a great trip and be safe...or else. -T.'"

Blake snorted.

He started the engine and pulled the car back onto the road, but I noticed he was being careful. He stayed (more or less) at the speed limit.

He put me in charge of choosing the music so, of course, I tuned in the car stereo to 102.5. Amelia Lockett was on the air. Blake had told me she and J.J. Jones were covering most of his shifts while we were away, so I felt a surge of appreciation for her, and for all of Blake's LOVE FM colleagues. I'd heard even his bosses had been incredibly supportive of him when he told them about this trip.

Reportedly, Doug and Leonard had exclaimed, "*Anything* for the sake of love."

Which was, in not so many words, almost exactly what Shar had said to me when I asked her to check in on Napoleon a few times over the weekend. Derek and Olivia were quick to agree to watching Winston so, really, the only thing Blake and I had to worry about was getting to the plane on time.

We talked for the whole drive, laughed, held hands. And, just as we reached the ramp to head into the airport, Barry Connelly's "You're the One" came on.

"Want me to change the station?" I asked. I remembered him saying how much he hated Connelly's music.

But Blake was full of surprises. "Nah," he replied. "This one is kinda growing on me."

And when I started singing along with it on the radio, Blake said with a laugh, "Oh, hell, this just might be our song." And he joined in.

~*END*~

UP NEXT: Look for Marianna's love story and her Sarasota, Florida adventure in *Stranger on the Shore*—coming soon!

EXCERPT: STRANGER ON THE SHORE (MIRABELLE HARBOR, BOOK 4) – COMING SPRING 2016!

On the verge of turning forty and having just lost her job, Marianna Gregory flees Mirabelle Harbor for the summer with little more than a suitcase, her beat-up car, and the blessings of her good friend Olivia Michaelsen. Her ex-husband is living a new life in California. Her college-aged daughter is spending her vacation with her boyfriend in Michigan. And the house Marianna once called her own finally sold, so she has nowhere to live in Illinois now anyway.

However, her wealthy sister Ellen owns an empty bungalow on the beach in Sarasota, Florida, so Marianna turns to the sea for a chance to go shelling, regroup, and figure out what to do with this new chapter in her life. She doesn't bargain on having to face down several family crises while she's away, nor does she count on meeting a handsome beachcomber who bears a striking resemblance to Elvis. Just as surprising is the craft project she gets roped into volunteering for and the new group of friends who might just change the way she views the world and her future.

The most unexpected gifts can be found where the land meets the sea. STRANGER ON THE SHORE, a Mirabelle Harbor story.

From the Novel:

"Here's your key," Mr. Niihau, the elderly proprietor of the Siesta Sunset bungalows, said to me, handing over a plastic keychain in the shape of a golden nautilus with a single key on the end. "It works for the laundry room, too."

I nodded and tried not to look as unenthusiastic about the idea of doing laundry as I felt. As hard as it was selling the house and, with it, the washer and drier that I'd scraped together enough cash to buy a year after Donny left me, I couldn't say I was going to *miss* the appliances all that much.

"Here are bath towels to get you started." He placed an assortment on the counter between us. "Garbage bags and a roll of paper towels." He added those and pointed in the direction of the narrow parking lot. "There should be extras of everything in your unit. Garbage pickup comes on Tuesdays. Throw your bags in the green dumpster at the end of the lot. And there's a big bin for recycling, too. Fresh sheets on Thursdays. Any questions?"

I inhaled and held the breath deep inside my chest for a moment. I was almost forty years old with no husband, no home of my own, and no paying job. My most pressing question was "Seriously, what am I gonna to do with my life?" but I did not ask Mr. Niihau this.

"Looks like I'm all set," I told him instead. "Thank you."

He smiled kindly, the corners of his eyes crinkling even further. The sun-weathered skin had seen seven decades at least, but he looked as though if someone were to say, "Surf's up!" he'd grab his board and race them to the water. My sister Ellen had told me he was born in Hawaii and still had the heart of an Islander. Having met him now, I totally believed that.

"Your sister's unit is number twenty-six," he reminded me. "Let me know if there's anything you need during your stay."

I assured him I would and, then, meandered down the outdoor walkway. The late-June humidity was so oppressive—good God! A person would be crazy to think Mirabelle Harbor was muggy by comparison. I felt wrapped in a in a tight wool blanket, the sweat being squeezed out of me, until I got to the shaded canopy of the bungalow that Ellen and her husband Jared bought as a vacation unit over a decade ago.

With the exception of a few weeks every winter, my sister and her husband didn't visit this property. They just rented it out through the year with the help of Mr. Niihau and his staff—often to an assortment of regulars and to some others, mostly families, who were looking for a place to stay on their beach holiday.

But not this summer.

For seven weeks, Ellen kept the reservation book clear for me. A gift for which I had no earthly idea how I might ever repay.

The door to unit #26 creaked as I unlocked it. I twisted the knob, pushed my way in and stepped inside a photograph.

I remembered this image exactly from a snapshot Ellen had sent one winter: A lush floral sofa with pretty buttercup throw pillows dominated the living room. A glass coffee table was parked in front of it. A small spotless kitchen was just beyond the front seating area with stainless steel appliances and a circular dining table jutting up against the main kitchen counter. A hallway could be found beyond that, with speckled tile floors throughout, an occasional throw rug and stark white walls dotted with a few small seascapes to break up the monotony.

The only difference between the photo in my memory and this room was that, in the former, my smart, successful older sister was lounging on the sofa, drinking from a 24-oz. ceramic mug of extra-strength coffee, and glancing up from her collection of work pages scattered on the glass table in front of her.

I had no such papers in my own bag, just an invisible, ever-growing list of differences between Ellen's life and mine. My sister's ability to do work while on vacation was only one of them.

My loafers click-clacked against the ceramic tiles as I strode down the hall to where the bedrooms were hidden. There were two available: One with a queen bed and one with a double. I opted for the larger of them—well, why the heck not?—and tossed my suitcase, purse, and jacket in the corner. The only items I retrieved from my bag were my flip-flops, which I slipped on after kicking off my travel loafers. Much like the way Mister Rogers changed his shoes at the start of his famous show when I was a kid, I felt the need to do the same.

I smoothed down a few wrinkles from my short-sleeve shirt and shorts and inhaled. Yes, I was about as comfortable as I could get under the circumstances. Ready to enter the Neighborhood of Make-Believe.

Check out the Mirabelle Harbor page on Marilyn's website for more information on the series: www.marilynbrant.com/books/the-mirabelle-harbor-series

OTHE NOVELS IN THE SERIES THAT ARE AVAILABLE NOW IN PAPERBACK & EBOOK:

TAKE A CHANCE ON ME (MIRABELLE HARBOR – BOOK 1)

Welcome to Mirabelle Harbor! In this scenic suburb on Chicago's North Shore, overlooking the sparkling waters of Lake Michigan, the Michaelsen family has made their home for generations. Although their parents and grandparents are now gone, siblings Derek, Blake, Sharlene, and the twins—Chandler and Chance—all have fond memories of growing up in town, and most still live there.

Chance Michaelsen, the youngest member of the family (by two minutes) and the quietest (by far), is a dedicated twenty-eight-year-old personal trainer at the local gym. While he might not say much, Chance has made it clear that he's not a fan of toxic people, unhealthy habits, or sharing too many of his emotions. With anybody.

Enter Antonia "Nia" Pappayiannis—the prettiest member of the loudest and most overly demonstrative family in town. They're also the owners of The Gala, a Greek restaurant and bakery known for its decadent pastries and located just a few steps from Chance's gym. He considers their entire family business to be the enemy of good health, but he can't quite shake his attraction to Nia, who doesn't seem nearly as impressed with him or his sculpted physique as most of the women around Mirabelle Harbor.

Unfortunately, between her doctor's orders and the interfering ways of Chance's crazy-making ex-girlfriend, who just happens to be one of Nia's long-time friends, Chance gets assigned to be Nia's fitness coach for the month. Pure torture. And if his ex weren't already causing enough problems, he also has to deal with Nia's current boyfriend—some hotshot Chicago CEO who talks big but, in Chance's opinion, is as fake as a Styrofoam barbell.

The road to romance is going to be a rocky one, and though Nia has her doubts about getting involved, Chance has a well-developed competitive streak and might just be willing to give it a shot...if he can convince her to do the same.

In matters of the heart, would you risk it all? TAKE A CHANCE ON ME, a Mirabelle Harbor story.

THE ONE THAT I WANT (MIRABELLE HARBOR, BOOK 2)

The summer after her beloved husband died in a car accident, Julia Meriwether Crane is still picking up the pieces of her life in Mirabelle Harbor and trying to help her ten-year-old daughter adjust to this difficult new reality.

After her best friend Sharlene—one of the well-connected Michaelsen siblings—talks her into finally going out on the town again, Julia finds herself stunned to be the object of interest of several different men: The boy who'd broken her heart back in high school. The college ex she'd left behind. And most surprising of all, the movie actor she'd always fantasized about but had never met in person...until now. Can one woman have more than one "great love" in the same lifetime? And, if so, how can she be sure which man that'll be?

Sometimes the person you think will be best for you isn't the one you really want. THE ONE THAT I WANT, a Mirabelle Harbor story.

ABOUT THE AUTHOR

Marilyn Brant has been told she writes with honesty, liveliness, and wit (descriptors she's grown terribly fond of) about complex, intelligent women—like her friends—and their significant personal relationships. Although her favorite pursuits undoubtedly involve books, she proves she's not just a literary snob by confessing her lifelong fascination (read: obsession) with popular music, especially from the '70s and '80s, most flavors of ice cream, and a variety of sensuous body lotions/oils.

As a former teacher, library staff member, freelance magazine writer, and national book reviewer, Marilyn has spent much of her life lost in literature. She is the *New York Times* and *USA Today* bestselling and award-winning author of twelve novels to date, and a lifetime member of the Jane Austen Society of North America. The Illinois Association of Teachers of English (IATE) selected her as their 2013 Author of the Year.

Her debut coming-of-age novel, *ACCORDING TO JANE* (Kensington, 2009), featuring the ghost of Jane Austen giving a young woman dating advice, won the Romance Writers of America's prestigious Golden Heart® Award and the Booksellers' Best, and it was named one of the "Top 100 Romance Novels of All Time" by Buzzle.com. Her second novel, *FRIDAY MORNINGS AT NINE* (Kensington, 2010), was a Doubleday and Book-of-the-Month Club pick in women's fiction. *A SUMMER IN EUROPE* (Kensington, 2011) was featured in the Literary Guild and BOMC2, and it became a Top 20 Bestseller in Fiction and Literature for the Rhapsody Book Club. The Polish translation of the novel was released in June 2013.

She's also a #1 Kindle and #1 Nook bestseller, who writes fun and flirty romantic comedies, like her stories in *THE SWEET TEMPTATIONS COLLECTION*, that involve sweet treats, unexpected love and large doses of humor. *THE ROAD TO YOU*—a coming-of-age romantic mystery—was selected as one of the Top 20 Best Books of the Year (December 2013) by The Reading Frenzy. Several of her novels are available in audio CD/download from Post Hypnotic Press. Be sure to keep an eye out for new upcoming romances in the "Mirabelle Harbor" series!

Marilyn currently lives in the Chicago suburbs with her family. When she isn't reading her friends' books or watching old movies, she's working on her next novel, eating chocolate indiscriminately and hiding from the laundry. Please visit her website: www.MarilynBrant.com.